INNOCENT
VICTIMS

INNOCENT VICTIMS

MINETTE WALTERS

The Mysterious Press
an imprint of Grove/Atlantic, Inc.
New York

FIRST AMERICAN EDITION

ISBN: 978-0-8021-2612-2

Chickenfeed was originally published in 2006 in the United Kingdom
by Macmillan.
The Tinder Box was originally published in 1999 by the United
Kingdom by Macmillan

The Mysterious Press
an imprint of Grove/Atlantic, Inc.
841 Broadway
New York, NY 10003

Distributed by Publishers Group West

www.groveatlantic.com

12 13 14 15 16   12 11 10 9 8 7 6 5 4 3 2 1

CONTENTS

AUTHOR'S NOTE

I hope you enjoy these novellas and find the contrast between them interesting. They were commissioned seven years apart, by two very different organizations, but the purpose behind them was the same: to encourage people to read.

The Tinder Box first appeared in Dutch translation under the title *De Tondeldoos*, and was given away free by the Organization for the Promotion of Books in the Netherlands during their 1999 Book Week. The aim was to persuade fluent readers to try a different genre, and upwards of half a million copies of *De Tondeldoos* were handed out on behalf of the crime genre.

Chickenfeed was published on World Book Day, 2006, as part of the first ever Quick Reads scheme in the UK. Quick Reads are designed to help non-fluent adult readers improve their literacy skills through access to grown-up ideas in easy-to-read language. The challenge to the author is to write a novella which appeals to all readers—experienced and inexperienced—so that the stories can be discussed by everyone. *Chickenfeed* was voted the Best Quick Read of 2006.

Both novellas explore the theme of justice. *The Tinder Box* depicts the dangers of prejudice within a small community, and how unrelated, misunderstood events combine to trigger a violent, vigilante reaction. *Chickenfeed* is a fictionalised retelling of the true story of the "Chicken Farm Murder" in Southern England in 1924 for which a young man was hanged.

Justice is as much about exonerating the innocent as it is about convicting the guilty, but the lines of responsibility become blurred when victims share the blame for what happens to them. How guilty is the perpetrator in those circumstances?

And how innocent the victim?

—Minette Walters

CHICKENFEED

Chickenfeed is based on the true story of the "Chicken Farm Murder," which took place in Blackness Road, Crowborough, East Sussex, in December 1924.

CHAPTER ONE

Kensal Rise Methodist Church,
*   north London—winter 1920*

The skies were dark with ice-filled clouds the day Elsie Cameron first spoke to Norman Thorne. Perhaps Elsie should have taken the gloom as an omen of what was to come. But could any girl predict that a man she met in church would hack her to pieces four years later in a place called Blackness Road?

Outside, the wind and sleet beat against the Gothic spire of the Kensal Rise church. Inside, the flock huddled in their coats and listened to the preacher. He thundered against the demon of drink, which stole a person's moral sense. Cursed would be the man who hit out in temper. Or the woman who had sex before marriage.

Elsie Cameron, a small, plain twenty-two-year-old with chewed fingernails and thick glasses, barely listened. She had heard it all before. It was a message of grinding despair to a lonely girl who suffered from depression. Elsie wanted to be loved. But the only love on offer in the chapel was God's, and His love came with conditions.

Her gaze slid sideways towards the young man who sat with his father and stepmother in a nearby pew. Each time Elsie saw him her heart beat a little faster. He was four years younger than she was—eighteen—but he was handsome and he always smiled if he caught her eye. His name was Norman Thorne and he worked as a mechanic at Fiat Motors in Wembley.

Norman's real mother had died when he was eight. At sixteen, he'd joined the Royal Naval Air Force to serve in the Great War. The war had ended three weeks after he arrived in Belgium and he never saw any fighting. But that didn't matter to Elsie. Any lad who stood up for his country was a hero.

She worried about the age difference because she had a fear of being teased. Would people call her a cradle-snatcher if she persuaded him to walk out with her? But his work as a mechanic had filled him out. No one would guess he was only eighteen. Elsie bit nervously at her fingernails as she tried to think of a way to speak to him.

Her mother had taught her that only "loose" women made the first move. Let the man come to you, she had said. But it hadn't worked. Elsie's brother and sister had no trouble finding girls and boys to "walk out" with. But not Elsie. Elsie scared would-be husbands away. She was too intense, too swamping, too desperate.

She feared the things she wanted, and wanted the things she feared. She had nightmares about being left on the shelf—unwanted and unloved—but she couldn't bring herself to flirt the way other girls did. The perfect man would be content to worship her until he put a ring on her finger. And only afterwards would anything of *that* sort happen.

There was a stubborn streak in Elsie's nature that blamed others for her problems. It wasn't her fault that she was plain. It was her *parents'* fault. And it wasn't her fault that she lacked friends. Only a fool would trust people who gossiped behind her back.

Elsie worked as a typist in a small firm in the City, but her colleagues had long since grown tired of her mood swings. They called her "difficult" and grumbled about her mistakes. She resented them for it. She resented her boss, who took her to task for failing to do her job properly.

Once in a while—in the depths of despair—she wondered if her co-workers were right. Was she difficult? More often, she blamed them for making her unhappy. If people were nice to her, she would be nice back. But why should *she* have to be nice first?

It's on such little things that life and death turn.

Would either have died if Norman hadn't smiled?

*   *   *

As the congregation filed out of church, Norman Thorne was a pace or two ahead of Elsie. Deliberately, she trod on the back of his heel while pretending to search through her bag. His startled face turned towards her.

She gave a squeak of dismay. "Whoops!" she exclaimed, clutching at his sleeve.

Norman put out his hand to steady her. "Are you all right?"

Elsie nodded. "I'm ever so sorry."

"Don't worry about it." He prepared to move on.

"I know who you are," she said in a rush. "Norman Thorne. I'm Elsie Cameron. We live quite close. My mum says you were in the war. That makes you a hero."

Norman gave a shy smile. "Not really."

"*I* think so."

The boy was flattered. And why not? He was young and no girl had ever looked at him this way before. Raised by a strict father, Norman neither drank nor smoked. He helped with the local Scouts, taught in the Sunday School and was involved in all kinds of chapel work.

His smile widened to one of welcome. "Nice to meet you, Elsie."

Norman's father wasn't pleased when his son told him he had a girl.

"You're too young for such nonsense," Mr. Thorne said. "You should put your energies into working."

"I'm not planning to marry her, Dad."

"Then watch how you treat her, lad. We don't want any shotgun weddings in this family."

Nor was Elsie's mother pleased. "He's still a boy, dear. You'd be better off with someone older."

"He doesn't look eighteen."

"Maybe not, Elsie . . . but he'll make you unhappy in the long run. He'll grow bored and leave you for someone else. Boys of that age always do."

Mrs. Cameron was bent over the kitchen sink, washing clothes. Her arms were deep in suds and Elsie stared at her stooped back with loathing. "Why do you always have to ruin everything for me?" she asked.

"I don't mean to," her mother said with a sigh, "but Dad and I both feel—" She broke off abruptly. She was too tired for arguments that day, and Elsie never took her advice anyway.

She had lost heart over the girl. There were no grey areas in Elsie's life. Love must be total. Support tireless. Fault-finding zero. Mild criticism, designed to help her, led to tantrums . . . or worse, threats of suicide. Elsie could go for weeks without speaking to either of her parents. Other times she fawned on them.

Conflict played a part in all her relationships. At home and at work. She could like a person one day and hate them the next. But she never understood why that turned people away. "It's not fair," she would say, bursting into tears. "Why is everyone so *beastly* to me?"

Neither of her parents could see a happy ending for her. Mrs. Cameron prayed she'd meet an older man who would put up with her moods. Mr. Cameron said no such man existed now. If he ever had, he'd died in the war.

The war had killed so many men. It meant a generation of young women would not find husbands. For every Norman Thorne, there were five young girls begging to be noticed. And Mrs. Cameron knew Elsie well enough to know that she was too needy to hold Norman's interest for long.

But, like her daughter's co-workers, she'd had enough of the petulant mood swings. "Do as you please," she said, drawing a pillowcase from the water and thumping it against the wooden washboard. "Just don't come running to me when Norman Thorne lets you down."

Chapter Two

North London—summer 1921

Norman scuffed his feet along the pavement. He'd been given his cards by Fiat and was living on ten shillings (50p) a week dole money. "Everyone's been laid off," he told Elsie. "It's happening all over. Dad says there's three million out of work and it's going to get worse."

Elsie had to walk fast to keep up with his longer legs. "What will you do?"

"I don't know."

"You'll have to do something, pet. You can't live on the dole forever."

(She meant: "If you don't find another job soon it'll be ages before we can marry." But as usual Norman dodged the issue.)

"We were lied to," he complained instead. "Us lads who went away to war were told we'd come home to 'a land fit for heroes.' Remember that? They promised us jobs and money"—he took a swipe at a bush as he passed—"and we haven't got bloody either."

Elsie let the "bloody" go. Now wasn't the time to take him to task for cursing. She felt like saying she was more upset than he was. Things had been going well while he was earning. So much so that her hints about marriage had brought a smile to his face. Then he lost his job and everything changed.

There could be no talk of weddings while he was out of work. Wives and children cost money. A man should never make promises he couldn't keep. There was more to marriage than kissing. Hardship and poverty led to anger and hate.

These weren't messages that Elsie wanted to hear. Her romantic streak said love could overcome all problems. What did it matter if they were poor as long as they had each other? She knew her feelings for Norman were stronger than his for her. She called him her "lovey," her "pet," her "treasure," but he only ever called her "Elsie" or "Else."

She tucked her hand through his arm and put on her brightest smile. "You're always telling me there's money in chickens. Why don't you start a chicken farm?"

"Where?" He sounded annoyed, as if he found her idea foolish. But he didn't push her away.

"Not in London. Somewhere outside. Sussex or Surrey maybe. Land's cheaper away from the city."

He slowed to a halt. "How would I pay for it?"

"You could ask your dad for a loan. You said he's been careful all these years. You never know. He might give you the money instead of making you wait till he's dead. He's got no one else to leave it to."

"Do you reckon?"

"I don't see why not. Raising chickens is better than living on the dole."

It was amazing how quickly his depression lifted. "You could be right, Else. He said he'd give me a hand if I needed it."

"There you are then."

He gave her fingers a quick squeeze. "We wouldn't see so much of each other. Sussex is a fair lick from Kensal Rise."

"We'll manage," she said. "We'll write every day. It'll make our love stronger."

Mr. Thorne surprised Norman by the speed with which he stumped up £100 for the project. Elsie said it was because he had faith in his son. But Norman thought it had more to do with parting him from Elsie. Mr. Thorne was a little too eager to see his boy move to Sussex. Perhaps he hoped that out of sight would mean out of mind.

"The change will do you good," he said cheerfully. "It's time you met new people and spread your wings. You're stuck in a rut here, lad."

Sometimes Norman felt that, too. He was fond of Elsie. He even wondered if he was in love with her when she was in a good mood. But he could never predict when that would be. It got him down. There were days when she was happy, and other days when she wasn't. But it was always him who had to match his mood to hers. Never the other way round.

She called her ups and downs her "nerves." "I worry about things, pet. It makes me jumpy. Mum says it'll wear off when I have a family. I can't be fretting for myself when I have children to look after."

Norman doubted that. Surely a baby would give her more to worry about? But he didn't say so. Elsie was easier to get on with when she was making plans. She took it for granted that her future would include him.

Once or twice, he tried to suggest differently. "I'm not the only bloke in the world, Else. Maybe you'll find someone better."

"How can I? You're my own sweet darling."

"Maybe *I'll* find someone better," Norman teased, not completely in jest.

She put him through hell when he said such things. An older man might have used the sulks as an excuse to end the affair. But not a church-going boy of nineteen who was both flattered and trapped by Elsie's devotion.

Which may explain why the idea of a chicken farm outside London was as welcome to Norman as it was to his father. He hoped a breathing space would help him make up his mind.

He bought a field off Blackness Road in Crowborough, Sussex, and took it over on August 22nd, 1921. In the hope of blessing the project from the start, he named the plot Wesley Poultry Farm. (John Wesley was the founder of the Methodist Church.)

Norman lodged locally. During the day he built chicken sheds and runs. The weather was warm in September and the work was hard. His only transport was his bicycle and he was careful what he spent.

After the purchase of land, he had to buy timber and wire, while keeping enough in reserve for chickens to stock the farm. It meant he spent most of his time alone and never treated himself to a night out.

Of course he missed Elsie. She wrote to him every day so that he wouldn't forget her. "My own darling Norman . . ." "Oh, my treasure, how I adore you . . ." "Do you think of me as much as I think of you, pet . . . ?" "Does absence make your heart grow fonder of your little lovey . . . ?"

It did. Every Friday evening he cycled the fifty miles to Kensal Rise to spend the weekend with her. But the round trip was tiring, and he warned her that he wouldn't be able to do it once the poultry arrived.

"I can't abandon them, Else. They'll need to be fed and watered Saturdays and Sundays, same as during the week."

She became tearful, so he told her he was planning to build a hut to live in. "It won't be much," he said. "Maybe twelve feet by eight feet, but there's a well for water and I can make a bed along one wall. I'll cook on an oil stove and light candles when it gets dark."

Elsie said it sounded romantic.

Norman shook his head. "It's the way the lads lived in the trenches," he told her. "Hard and rough . . . but it'll be cheaper than paying for a room every night. I'll add to it as things get better and one day it'll be a proper house."

She was already thinking ahead. "I can visit at weekends."

"It's not built yet."

"I'll come down by train and walk from the station."

"You won't be able to stay overnight, Elsie. It'll look bad."

"I know." She gave his arm a teasing punch. "Silly boy! I'll sleep in lodgings and spend the days with you. We'll have fun, pet. I'll do the cooking while you look after the chickens. We can pretend we're married."

It did seem romantic when she put it like that. And Norman *was* lonely. Sussex folk were wary of strangers and the new friends his father had promised had never appeared. So far, his only reward for "spreading his wings" was hard work. And hard work was joyless when there was no one to share it with.

In any case, he was a healthy young man. He still had strong chapel views, but the thought of being alone with a woman excited him.

He built his live-in shack to the same design as his hen houses. The walls were made of wood and a high-pitched roof gave a feeling of space inside. Two beams, one above the other, ran across the centre to hold the structure rigid. At one end, a mattress on a platform served as a bed at night and a sofa during the day. At the other end, a small window let in some light.

He furnished the room with bits and pieces to make it more homely. A table and two chairs, an oil stove, a tin bowl for washing, and some matting on the floor. But, otherwise, it was just as he had promised Elsie. Rough, hard living. Made worse by the cold as the days shortened and winter drew in.

He refused to let Elsie visit until the spring of 1922. "The weather's too bad," he wrote to her. "It's hard to keep warm and most days I don't bother to wash. I sometimes think the chickens are better off than me. At least they can huddle together."

He kept from her that the farm wasn't going well. Few of his hens were laying. Some were too young, some were off-lay, but most were affected by the rain. A local man warned him that the weather might stop the birds producing eggs for two months.

Norman was shocked. "I can't afford to wait that long," he said. "I need something to sell. I'm living from hand to mouth as it is."

The man shrugged. "It was a bad time to start a poultry farm, lad. Chickens don't like the winter. Eggs are scarce now, but you'll have more than you can sell when the spring comes. You'll be lucky to cover the cost of the chickenfeed."

"What will I live on?"

"Eggs?" the man suggested with dry humour. "You'll come to hate the taste of them . . . but they'll keep the wolf from the door."

CHAPTER THREE

Wesley Poultry Farm,
Blackness Road—summer 1922

Elsie loved Norman's little shack. She'd never been so happy as on the weekends that she spent at the farm. She took a room down the road with Mr. and Mrs. Cosham, and walked to the field every day. She helped with the feeding and the collecting of eggs, but she wouldn't clean out the hen houses.

"The smell makes me sick," she told Norman, wrinkling her nose. "And I can't go back to London reeking of chicken mess."

Norman didn't mind. He was content to let Elsie sit and do nothing as long as she was there. Her joy rubbed off on him and he began to think the project could work after all. True, he was producing more eggs than he could trade, but the cockerels and the broody hens were doing their jobs well. He now had plenty of young chicks to fatten and sell for the pot.

Elsie asked him how he was going to kill them.

"Break their necks," he said.

"Dad says his mother in Scotland did it with a knife."

"I don't want blood on the neck feathers."

"Won't you have to pluck them, lovey? Who's going to buy a chicken that's not been plucked?"

"It's only the bodies that need doing, Else. You leave the heads and neck as they are so the butcher can hang them in his window. They don't look so good with blood on them."

She squatted down to stare at a clutch of fluffy chicks. "Poor little things."

"Poor me, more like," said Norman. "I'll be plucking in my sleep if the business takes off. The feathers come out pretty easily if the bird's still warm, but it's hard work even so."

"There'll be a lot of feathers, pet. What will you do with them?"

"I don't know," he said, looking around the field. "Burn them maybe. It'll make the place stink for a while but at least I'll be rid of them."

He had more of a problem with soiled straw from the chicken sheds. He was rotting it down to sell as compost, but the process took time. Meanwhile, the growing heaps made the farm look even more run-down and tatty than it was. At first, Elsie didn't seem to notice. But after a few weeks she began to nag him about it.

"No one's going to buy your eggs if they've seen where they come from. They'll *expect* them to be bad. You need to paint the sheds. Make them look clean."

"I can't afford to," he said crossly. "Paint costs money."

"Ask your dad for more."

"He's given me enough already."

When her nagging became too much, he suggested *she* give him the money to buy paint. "You say you want us to be wed, Elsie, but it won't happen if the farm fails. I know you've got savings. It won't break the bank to lend me a few quid, will it?"

"My dad will have my hide if I lend money to a man I'm not engaged to," she said coyly. "You'll have to put a ring on my finger first, pet."

"And what will I buy it with? Do you know a jeweller who'll trade diamonds for poultry?"

But in spite of the odd argument about money and marriage, the summer and autumn passed happily enough. September and October were warm, and Elsie came down to Sussex almost every weekend. On Saturdays she and Norman lazed by a fire outside the hut when their tasks were over. On Sunday mornings they walked to the Methodist chapel in the centre of town before returning home to a meal made by Elsie.

She became expert at finding different ways to cook chicken. As often as not, the bird was an old one that needed boiling with carrots and onions. But for treats Norman would kill a young cockerel that could be fried in bacon lard from the local pig farm. It was more like camping than keeping proper house, but, as Elsie was fond of saying, "It's like being on holiday."

Norman's father had told him once that holidays were the worst time to fall in love. "People act differently when they're away from home, son. You can't judge a lass by the way she is at the seaside."

Norman wondered about that every time Elsie talked of marriage. Which was the real Elsie Cameron? The intense, nervy one who lived with her parents in London and hated her job? Or the carefree one who visited him in Sussex and played at being a wife? He knew she thought about sex almost as often as he did. Sometimes they came close to doing it.

He would pull her to him, clasping her buttocks and thrusting his hard penis against the folds of her skirt. There was always a second or two before she giggled and pushed him away.

"Naughty boy!" she'd say, wiggling her ring finger under his nose. "You'll have to get down on your knees and propose to me, Norman. Promise to make me Mrs. Thorne and I might think about it."

"As soon as I make ends meet."

"And when's that going to be?"

"I don't know. I'm doing my best."

"That's all you ever say. If you loved me as much as I love you, you'd sweep me in your arms and propose anyway. I don't mind living in a hut."

"You would if it was every day, Elsie. It's no holiday, believe me. If I can't get a butcher to take my birds, I have to go house to house to sell the flaming things. And no one pays full price . . . not when they see how desperate I am to be rid of them. A dead hen doesn't last long."

There was no point bringing them home. The only place to hang dead birds was from the beam in his shed and they rotted quickly in the heat. On the two or three times that he'd tried it, he'd ended up burying the corpses in the field. No one wanted poultry that wasn't fresh. Worse, the smell of death attracted foxes and rats.

There were no easy answers to his money problems. He'd been foolish to start the project without learning more about farming. But there was no going back now. He kept telling himself it would come right in the end. He'd been taught that God takes care of those who take care of themselves. And that hard work wins its own reward. But worry gnawed at his gut all the time.

What if it wasn't true? What if God was teaching him a lesson in humility? How could he explain the waste of £100 to his father? How could he explain to Elsie that he might *never* be in a position to marry her?

He was always at his lowest in the hours before dawn. He lay awake, seeing himself in a trap of his own making. If he hadn't met Elsie . . . if he hadn't asked his father for money . . . if Elsie had been younger and less desperate to get married . . .

They became engaged on Christmas Day, 1922. Norman left the feeding of his birds to Mr. Cosham and cycled back to London for the holiday. He told his father he was doing well enough to propose to Elsie Cameron.

Mr. Thorne frowned at him. "Are you sure, son? The last I heard you were living in a wooden hut. Is that still the case?"

"Yes."

"Are you expecting a wife to live in it with you?"

"We're just getting engaged, Dad. The wedding won't be for a while yet, and by then I'll have found a place to rent."

"Mm. Whose idea was it? Yours or Miss Cameron's?"

A stubborn look came over Norman's face. "Mine."

Mr. Thorne didn't believe him. "Will it make a difference if I refuse to give you my blessing? I quite see why Miss

Cameron wants a husband—she's nearly twenty-five—but you're only twenty, lad. Much too young to start a family."

"We aren't planning to have children straight away."

"*You* might not be, boy, but I'm sure Miss Cameron is."

Norman gritted his teeth. "I'm not a boy any more, Dad, and her name's Elsie. I wish you could see her the way I do. She's sweet and kind and only wants what's best for me."

"So do I, Norman."

"It doesn't seem like it sometimes."

Mr. Thorne eyed him for a moment. "Has Elsie given you a hundred pounds?"

"No."

"Then don't accuse me of not caring."

"I'm not," said his son unhappily, "but life isn't just about money, Dad."

Mr. Thorne shook his head. "It is when you sign up for something you can't afford. There's no time for love when the bailiffs come knocking on your door."

How different it was in the Cameron household. Elsie's father clapped Norman on the back and told him he was a grand fellow. "Our girl's always wanted to be wed. She had one of her turns when her brother and sister both got engaged this year. But all's well that ends well, eh? We're glad to have you as a son."

Mrs. Cameron hugged him. "You're a good boy, Norman. I knew you'd offer sooner or later. Our Elsie's that keen to start a family."

Norman gave a sheepish smile. "It'll be a while yet, Mrs. Cameron. We need to find a place to live first."

Elsie tucked her hand through his arm and stretched out her finger so that the firelight flashed on her ring. "Not that long, pet. If you can give this to your girl, you can find a little house for her, can't you?"

Norman thought guiltily of the five pounds he'd borrowed from a moneylender to purchase the ring. "Maybe next year."

He was talking about twelve months hence, 1924, but the Camerons assumed he meant 1923. Elsie's brother and sister planned to wed that year, and it seemed fitting that she should, too. For the whole of Christmas Day, the chat was of nothing but bridal gowns and babies.

It was this that prompted Norman to bury his head in the sand. It was easier to agree than keep pointing out that he couldn't afford a wife and family just yet. He even became a little alarmed at how keen Mr. and Mrs. Cameron were to be rid of their daughter.

"She'll settle down once she's away from London," Mrs. Cameron said. "It's the noise and the crowds that make her depressed. Try not to keep her waiting too long, Norman."

Mr. Cameron took him aside after lunch. "Elsie gets bees in her bonnet . . . but you know that already. My advice is not to cross her. She's better when she has her own way."

"I'll do my best, sir."

"Good man. If you can see your way to tying the knot before her brother and sister do, you'll make her the happiest girl on earth."

Norman knew that wasn't possible but he didn't say so. In the naive way of a twenty-year-old, he hoped the issue would go away. He thought he could stall forever as long as a date wasn't fixed.

No one could force a bloke to marry before he was ready.

> 86 Clifford Gardens
> Kensal Rise
> London

January 30th, 1923

My own darling Norman,

The <u>worst</u> has happened. Mr. Hanley sacked me today, so your little Elsie has no job any more. He was <u>that</u> beastly, lovey. He said he was letting me go for the sake of the others. They've been telling lies about me again, and all because they can't bear to see me happy. They're jealous of my ring and jealous that I'm engaged. I really <u>hate</u> them.

Dad says I must look for another position but I won't need to if we can marry soon. Please say we can. I can't wait to be your wife, pet. I could find work as a typist in town and come home to the hut every night. We'll manage fine if I promise not to have babies for a year or two.

Oh, my darling, I love you so much. Please, please say yes.

Your own true sweetheart,

Elsie xxx

Blackness Road
Crowborough
Sussex

February 3rd, 1923

My dear Elsie,

I'm sorry you've lost your job but I think your father's right. You must look for another post in London. The hut's no place to live and a wife can't promise not to have babies. They happen whether you like it or not.

It's so cold at the moment that the hens' drinking water turns to ice every night. I have to sleep in my overcoat so that I don't freeze too. You wouldn't like it at all. And no one will employ a typist who can't wash herself or her clothes properly.

Patience is a virtue, Else. If we wed now we won't be as happy as if we wait. For that reason I'm sure it's better to delay.

Here's hoping you find a new job soon.

Your loving,

Norman

CHAPTER FOUR

Wesley Poultry Farm,
Blackness Road—summer 1923

Norman was coming to dread Elsie's weekend visits. Her happiness of the previous year had given way to bouts of anger and depression. She nagged him about everything. His refusal to name a day. His lack of money. Her endless misery, which she said was his fault.

Suddenly, she was unable to hold down a job. After working for the same firm for nine years, she had now been given her cards three times in five months. That, too, she blamed on Norman.

"They keep asking when I'm going to be wed and I can't tell them," she said. "They laugh at me behind my back."

"I'm sure they don't, Else. Everyone knows you have to save a bit before you can get hitched. There's loads of lads and lasses in the same boat as us."

She stamped her foot. "They *do* mock me . . . and I hate them for it. I can't work in a place where people give me nasty looks all the time."

"Are you sure it's not you who starts it? If you glare at someone, they'll glare back. Stands to reason."

But it was better not to say such things. As Mr. Cameron had remarked, his daughter was happier when she had her own way. And "having her own way" meant that Norman must agree with whatever she said. Nothing in life was Elsie's fault. If things went wrong for her, it was other people who should take the blame.

Sometimes Norman believed it. He felt guilty about raising her hopes then dashing them again. But if he hadn't proposed, she'd have been even more unhappy. A ring was proof that he loved her. It was also permission to touch her body.

Was this one of the reasons why he had begun to dread her visits? It was no longer a case of thrusting against her skirt. When she was in the mood, she let him take her clothes off and feel her naked skin. But that was as far as he was allowed to go. Showing he could control his urges was yet more proof that he loved her.

"I'm keeping myself for our wedding night, pet. A wife must be pure in body and mind when her husband enters her for the first time. You can do all sorts of other things but you can't put *that* in my body. *That* would be wrong."

He dreamt about her when she wasn't there, and became angry when she was. "You're a cock-teaser," he would growl every time she pushed him away. "You can't get a chap worked up then tell him to take a cold bath. I've got rubbers. Why can't we use them?"

"They're vulgar."

"Who cares?"

"I don't want to talk about it."

"All right, we won't use rubbers. I've promised to marry you so what are you scared of? I'm not going to let you down."

"You have so far," she would say huffily, stepping into her dress and pulling it up. "If you fixed a date, it might be different, but I'm not giving myself to you for a cheap ring."

"That's not what you said last summer. Last summer you said you'd think about it if I promised to make you Mrs. Thorne."

"Then make me Mrs. Thorne."

"What's the point? You'll just come up with another excuse. How do I know you'll ever do it, Else?"

"I want a baby, don't I?"

"And what happens when you have it? I sometimes think all you want is a new pet to moon over."

These were sterile arguments that went nowhere and only served to make them angry with each other. Both were sexually frustrated. Norman tried to deal with it by working harder. Elsie swung between moods of dark depression and moods of starry-eyed romance which she put into her love letters from London.

> Oh, my dearest Darling . . . our romance is like a fairy tale and it will end with "They lived happily ever after" . . . How I adore you, my treasure . . . you mean everything to me. I know we can manage in your little hut . . . and Elsie promises to love you always . . . Oh, my Darling, you cannot realise what you mean to me . . . I dream of the day we are together. For ever and ever, your own true sweetheart, Elsie.

Norman didn't know what to make of such letters. It seemed to him that, safely back in London, she reinvented herself as a princess in a fairy story. She forgot the hardship of the farm and saw it instead as a place of beauty. But how would he ever make her happy when the reality—mud, smell and debt—was so different?

The ups and downs of the relationship were taking their toll on Norman. More so, his never-ending money worries. Try as he might, he could not balance his books.

He was up against farmers on long-established contracts, and there was no demand for Wesley chickens and eggs. Had he planned the project better, he would have toured the area and counted the number of poultry farms. Or the number of houses that kept hens in their gardens. As it was, he'd bought the field on Blackness Road blindly.

He ran up debts with the chickenfeed producers. Then borrowed to pay them off. He told himself it was money well spent if it produced a profit in the end. All he needed was one good deal with a butcher for a regular supply of birds every week.

But his father's words haunted him. "There's no time for love when the bailiffs come knocking on your door."

As 1923 moved on towards Christmas, Elsie became more and more desperate. She'd been out of work for months, and her brother and sister had married and left her alone with her parents. Now Mr. and Mrs. Cameron were on Norman's back as well. They were as single-minded as their daughter. When was he going to make an honest woman of Elsie?

They might just as well have said: "When are you going to take Elsie off our hands?" For that's how Norman saw it. The more he avoided fixing a date, the harder Elsie's parents pressed him.

"You're breaking our girl's heart," said Mr. Cameron coldly on Christmas Day. "May I remind you that it's now twelve months since you put a ring on her finger."

"I know that, sir." Norman took a deep breath to calm himself. "But as I've explained several times I'm not in a position to marry at the moment. I need—"

Mr. Cameron broke in. "Why did you make a promise if you weren't prepared to keep it?"

I wasn't given a choice . . . Elsie forced me into it . . . I should have listened to my father . . . "I thought the farm would come good this year."

"And it hasn't?"

"It's only a matter of months, sir. If you could persuade Elsie to wait a little bit longer—"

"It's not my duty to persuade Elsie of anything," Mr. Cameron snapped. "As I see it, my only duty is to remind you that you are legally bound to marry her . . . or be taken to court for breach of promise."

A sullen expression settled on Norman's face. "It was Elsie who wanted the ring. I was happy as we were. In any case, I haven't said I'm not willing to go through with it. I'm just asking for a little more time."

"Which Elsie doesn't have, Norman. She'll be twenty-six in April."

"She doesn't look it."

"That's not the point though, is it? She feels life is passing her by. Her brother and sister are wed now." Mr. Cameron sighed. "She says people laugh at her because she's on the shelf."

MINETTE WALTERS

Norman felt a twinge of pity for the man. He knew how difficult Elsie could be when she thought she was being mocked. But his pity was short lived because he blamed both Mr. and Mrs. Cameron for the way Elsie was. If they hadn't spoilt her by giving way to her every mood, she wouldn't have thrown so many tantrums.

Yet the truth was he did the same himself. What else could a bloke do when his girl sulked and wept and said she was going to kill herself?

His own father was quick to notice his waning interest. "You're home early," he said, glancing at his watch on Christmas afternoon when Norman joined him in the front parlour. "Not spending the evening with Elsie?"

"No." Norman took a chair beside the fire. "I need an early night. I have to cycle back tomorrow."

"I thought you were staying longer."

"Changed my mind."

Mr. Thorne eyed him for a moment. "Have you and Elsie fallen out?"

"Not really."

"Then what's the problem?"

"The usual. I can't afford to get married yet."

A short silence fell between them.

"Is that the real reason you're putting the wedding off?" Mr. Thorne asked then.

"What other reason would there be?"

"You're not in love with her any more." He leaned forward to look at his son. "If so, it would be kinder to be honest with her now . . . give her a chance to find someone else."

"She doesn't want anyone else, Dad. She's mad about me. Says she'll kill herself if I ever let her down. She has these black moods when she thinks the whole world's against her." He dropped his hands between his knees and picked at some fluff on the carpet. "Mr. Cameron says he'll sue me for breach of promise if I don't marry her."

Mr. Thorne smiled slightly. "I wouldn't let that scare you. It's an idle threat. No one takes a man to court unless there's money to be made out of him. And you don't have any."

"I don't want to treat her badly, Dad. I'm still fond of her."

"I'm sure you are, son. But it would be cruel to marry her . . . then spend the rest of your life wishing you hadn't."

The idea that it would be kinder to let Elsie down gently took root in Norman's mind. He told her not to visit because of the winter cold and wrote fewer letters to her. Those he sent were cool and formal, and contained no expressions of love. He hoped she'd take the hint and give up of her own accord.

She didn't.

As his ardour cooled, Elsie's grew. Her replies were full of passion—"I adore you . . . I worship you . . . I can't wait for the spring . . ." It was as if she thought the power of her feelings could scorch through the page into Norman's heart. How could any man fail to respond to a woman who loved him so deeply?

As often as not, Norman left the letters unopened. Just the sight of her handwriting on the envelope set his teeth on edge. He was unable to deal with so much emotion. He felt swamped and oppressed by the false picture Elsie painted of him.

He was a failed chicken farmer with mounting debts who found his fiancée tiresome. So why did she keep calling him her "clever darling husband" and herself "his true little wife"?

As soon as the weather improved, she came down to the farm for a weekend. He tried to tell her that he wanted the relationship to end. But she became hysterical, stamping her feet and hissing abuse.

"I don't *want* to talk. Do you think I'm stupid? Do you think I don't know what's going on?"

Norman shook his head guiltily. "What do you mean?"

"Look at the sheets," she spat. "You've had other women in them." She pulled the bedclothes off and kicked them against the wall. "They're *dirty. You're* dirty." Her thin body quivered with anger. "You've been doing things on our special place. It's *hateful . . . disgusting.*"

He stared at her open-mouthed. "You're crazy! I don't know any other women . . . not to kiss and cuddle, anyway."

"What about *prostitutes?*" she screamed. "You're wasting your money on *sluts*, Norman. I *know* you are! That's why you never have any money."

"You need your head seeing to, Elsie," he said in disgust.

She burst into a storm of tears and flung herself against his chest. "I'm sorry . . . I'm sorry, pet. You don't know what it's like being away from you. I get so depressed. I get so *jealous.*"

He gave her an awkward hug. "There's nothing to be jealous about."

"But I don't know that," she said, wrapping her thin arms round his waist. "I keep thinking of you doing to other girls what you do to me. It's nice, darling. I *like* it." She pulled him against her. "You like it, too. *See.*"

39

She tried to guide his hand towards her breast, but he pulled away sharply as if she'd given him an electric shock. "Don't," he said harshly.

"Why not?"

"It's not right."

Her eyes glittered angrily behind her glasses. "You were happy to do it last year. You can't mess with me then pretend it didn't happen, Norman. I'm not some cheap tart you can throw over when you get bored. I'm the woman you're going to marry."

He headed for the door. "I have to clean the chicken sheds," he muttered. "We'll talk later."

Norman threw himself into work as a way to avoid contact. Elsie watched listlessly from the shack doorway. He couldn't decide what to do. Tell her outright that it was over? Or keep hoping that she would take the hint herself? Surely even Elsie—despite her strangeness—must see there was nothing to be gained by marrying a man who didn't love her?

But when the evening came, she behaved as if nothing had happened. The bed was remade, and Norman was her "own dear darling" again. It was as if she had spent the whole day working out how to win back his favour. No angry looks. No stamping. No touching. Just healthy cooking and lots of light laugher . . . plus an endless stream of fond words.

In an odd sort of way it made Norman feel more abused than if she had forced herself on him. For it suggested that he was shallow and uncaring. Did she really believe that all he thought about was his stomach? And that food should be served with smiles and silly endearments?

By the time he walked her to the station on Sunday afternoon, he was close to strangling her. Why couldn't she see how much she repulsed him? More than anything he *hated* the feel of her coarse, chewed fingertips against his skin.

Chapter Five

Crowborough—summer 1924

Norman met Bessie Coldicott at a local dance that Whitsun. It was shortly after the weekend with Elsie. Bessie was everything Elsie wasn't. She was young. She was pretty. She was warm and understanding. And she enjoyed flirting. Best of all, she accepted Norman for what he was. A young man who was struggling to make a living in difficult times.

He loved the way she made no demands on him. With no fear of being left on the shelf, she was content to chatter about anything that didn't include wedding bells. Suddenly Norman could be the person he wanted to be. A bit of a lad. A bit of a joker.

It was a rebirth. Instead of the morose silences that had begun to mark his relationship with Elsie, he could be witty and funny with Bessie. They started walking out together within a week of the dance.

"Am I your first girl?" she asked him one day.

"No."

"What were the others like?"

"Not a patch on you. The first one looked like a horse." He grinned. "The second one looked like a horse's arse."

Bessie danced away from him. "I don't believe you. I bet they were pretty and I bet you've had more than two. A bloke can have his pick these days."

"I was a slow starter . . . but I'm catching up now." He ran after her and caught her round the waist. "Like this." He planted a kiss on her full, soft lips.

Her eyes flashed with mischief. "Don't go getting ideas, Norman Thorne. I've plenty of other admirers and there's some I like just as well as you."

He knew it. All men found Bessie attractive. It was part of her appeal for him. The chase. The thrill of trying to win her. If other men had looked at Elsie in the way they looked at Bessie, he might have prized her more. But Elsie had never turned a head in her life.

Each time one of Elsie's letters arrived, Norman felt twinges of guilt about keeping her dangling. But like all cheats he put his own happiness first. On the two or three weekends that Elsie came to the farm during the summer, he managed to jolly her through them without too many rows. Her moods had less impact when he knew he could laugh with Bessie after she was gone.

His hardest task was keeping Elsie at bay in the shack. She was at him all the time, rubbing against him and urging him to undress her the way he used to. She told him she'd changed.

"I'm not afraid to have sex any more, pet," she coaxed. "It's natural when two people love each other."

"What if you get pregnant?"

"You can use a rubber if you want."

"I don't have them any more," he lied. "I threw them away. In any case, it's too dangerous, Else. Your dad'll give you hell if you end up with a baby out of wedlock."

"I don't care, lovey. I want to show you how much you mean to me. And how can I do that unless I give myself to you?" Tears welled in her eyes. "Please let's do it, Norman. You need to know what a good wife I'll be."

He was canny enough to recognize that this wasn't her real reason for wanting sex. He began to see their relationship like a game of chess. Each of them was trying to force the other into a corner. Norman wanted Elsie to realize she had no future with him. While Elsie wanted to bind Norman to her by getting pregnant.

* * *

In the dark hours of the night, Norman often tried to convince himself that he should marry Elsie. "Better the devil you know than the devil you don't," he'd say out loud.

He'd shared his life with her for four years. She knew more about him than any other person on earth. There were even times when the thought of her not being there scared him. Perhaps he'd grow tired of Bessie, too.

Sometimes he wondered if he cared for women at all. His chickens gave him more affection than people did. It still upset him to break their necks and remove their pretty plumage.

He loved the way they ran when he called to them. Necks stretched out and legs pumping. The young ones scampered so fast they fell over his feet as he walked towards them. He had to tread carefully. Some were tame enough to be stroked, others skittered away with nervous cheeps.

He had one cockerel who was a fighter. A Welsummer with blue-black tail feathers and a magnificent red comb. Norman called him Satan because of the evil that lurked in his beady eyes. If a cockerel in the next-door run strayed too close, Satan leapt at the wire and tried to attack him. He guarded his own hens jealously. Norman admired him for it.

He also admired Satan's appetite for sex, which meant few of his hens produced unfertilized eggs. This was in contrast to his Buff Orpington and Leghorn cockerels, whose milder natures made them lazy.

Which wasn't to say that Norman liked Satan. He treated him as warily as a snake after the bird attacked him from behind one time. Satan drove his sharp spurs into the back of Norman's leg and the wound hurt for days.

"I don't know why you don't kill him," said Elsie.

"What for?"

"Teach him a lesson."

"What's he going to learn when he's dead? And what good would it do me? Only a madman would kill his best cockerel."

"Then teach the others a lesson."

Norman looked at her with irritation. "They're chickens, Elsie. Their brains are about *this* big." He made a tiny gap between his thumb and forefinger. "They learn where their food is and they learn to lay their eggs in the nesting boxes. But that's *it*."

"There's no need to get snappy with me. I was only trying to help."

"Yes, well . . . it's a stupid idea. It was my mistake anyway. I got him riled. It makes him jealous when his hens eat out of my hand."

"His brain can't be *that* small then," she said acidly. "Isn't jealousy what *humans* feel?"

Norman's irritation grew. "How would I know?" he asked unkindly. "I've never had anything to feel jealous about."

He was lying, of course. He was jealous of any man who could bring a smile to Bessie Coldicott's face. She was a dressmaker in Crowborough and he took to hanging around outside the shop where she worked.

She teased him about it. "How come you go down my street so often? The nearest butcher's two roads away."

"It's a short cut."

"Fibber!" She tapped him lightly on the wrist. "You'll get me in trouble if you do it too often. Mrs. Smith's a nice lady but she doesn't like men peering through the window. It upsets the clients."

"I just want to say hello sometimes."

She laughed. "But not when I'm working, Norman. I like my job and I don't want to lose it. You can meet me at the back when I finish of an evening. Then walk me home afterwards."

As the summer passed, he spent more and more time with her. He asked her repeatedly to visit the farm but she always refused. "You live on your own, Norman. What would people say?"

"Who's going to see you? It's in the middle of nowhere."

"Someone will. Bored old ladies peep through their curtains to spy on their neighbours. Everyone talks in a place like this."

He wondered if she knew about Elsie. "What do they say?"

"That you had a girl visit a few times. Is that true?"

He'd always known it would come out in the end. He took a deep breath. "Yes, but there was nothing wrong about it, Bessie. She never stayed in the shack. It was all above board and proper."

"Who is she?"

"Someone I know from London. I was keen on her once but not any more. The trouble is—" He broke off. "She's a bit of a loony. Acts weird all the time . . . shouting and yelling one minute, crying the next. She keeps being given the sack because of it."

Bessie pulled a face. "There's a woman like that in our street. She bursts into tears if anyone speaks to her. Dad says it's because she lost two sons in the war, but Mum says she was born weird. She used to do it before they died."

"Elsie's always been strange."

"Is that her name?"

Norman nodded. "Elsie Cameron. It was mostly her parents' idea that she came to visit. I reckon they hoped I'd marry her and take her off their hands. She's a lot older than me and they're fed up with looking after her."

"That's horrible."

Yes, thought Norman. It *was* horrible. Why should he be expected to make Mr. and Mrs. Cameron's life easier by marrying their mad daughter? *He* hadn't given birth to her. *He* hadn't spoilt her.

He reached for Bessie's hand. "Don't worry, pet. It's not going to happen. I've loads of plans for the future . . . and none of them includes Elsie."

"What about me? Am I in your plans?"

"Maybe."

She gave his fingers a sharp pinch. "Then don't call me 'pet,' Norman. I'm not a fluffy chick to be kissed and stroked when you're in the mood. I'm me—and I don't belong to anyone."

Chapter Six

Wesley Poultry Farm,
*   Blackness Road—autumn 1924*

Bessie came to tea at the beginning of September. She gave Norman twenty-four hours' notice and he spent the night and morning cleaning the shack. He couldn't believe how filthy it was. The floor was covered in chicken shit from his boots, and dust lay everywhere.

Appalled at the state of his sheets, he went into town and bought new ones. It left him short of money but he didn't think Bessie would sit on a bed that stank of sweat and grime. He folded the dirty sheets and hid them in an empty nesting box. He planned to swap them back before Elsie's next visit in case she guessed that another woman had visited.

His hard work paid off. Bessie was impressed by the hut. "It's quite cosy. How long have you been living here?"

"Two years."

"Don't you get cold?"

"I do in the winter."

She looked at the beam above her head where he stored his hats. "That's neat. Where do you keep your clothes?"

"Behind here." He lifted a curtain that was nailed to one wall. "They're hung on pegs and this keeps the dust off them."

"Neat," she said again. "What's in here?" She pointed to a small chest of drawers.

Norman's heart skipped a beat. *Elsie's love letters.* He should have hidden them along with the sheets. "Razors . . . nail scissors . . . stuff that men use."

She sat on the edge of the bed. "It's better than I thought it would be. I was expecting something tatty."

"Why?"

"Because you call it a shack. I thought it'd be built out of tin . . . or bits of old iron." She patted the mattress. "If you'd told me it was like this, I might have come sooner."

He couldn't tell if she was giving him a come-on. Because of Elsie's moods he found women's signals confusing. Was Bessie inviting him to sit on the bed with her? Was she inviting him to go further? Or was it a test to see how much of a gentleman he was?

He bent to light the oil stove beneath the kettle. "Where would you like your tea?" he asked.

"Outside," she said with a smile. "It's warm in the sunshine." She pushed herself upright and walked to the door. "We'll have it inside when the days turn colder."

After that, Norman's life moved out of his control. Bessie started visiting the shack every night after work. And with none of Elsie's rigid views about rubbers and wedding bells, it wasn't long before they were having sex. The contrast between her softly welcoming arms and Elsie's cold, stiff fear could not have been greater.

How could he *ever* have fallen for Elsie?

He tried to gear himself up to tell her the truth. He wrote letters that he never sent. He even went to London at the start of October to say the words to her face. "It's over, Elsie. I don't love you any more. There's someone else."

He couldn't do it. She clung to him like a limpet, smiling for no reason. When he accused her of being drunk, she laughed.

"No, silly," she said fondly. "The doctor's put me on tablets for my nerves."

"What kind of tablets?"

She pulled a bottle from her bag. "I don't know but they're making me better. I've stopped fretting about things so much."

Norman read the label. "What the heck are 'sedatives,' Else?"

"I don't know," she said again. "But I'm quite well now. We can get married whenever you like."

"That's not—"

"We'll talk about it when I come down at the end of the month," she said happily. "It's all planned. I've already written to Mr. and Mrs. Cosham to book a room. We'll have such fun, pet."

"But—" He stopped.

"But what, pet?"

"It'll be cold," he said lamely.

Norman told Bessie it was his father who was coming to stay. "He wants to see for himself how the farm's going," he lied. "I owe it to him, Bess. He gave me the money to get started."

"So why don't you want me to meet him?"

"I do . . . just not yet. I've told him I'm working every hour God gave to get the business off the ground."

"Are you ashamed of me, Norman?"

"Course not. But what's he going to think if he sees you here? He'll know I can't keep my hands off you."

Bessie rolled on to her side to look at him. "That's true. You're worse than Satan."

Norman grinned. "Except Satan does it with all the hens . . . and I only do it with one."

She touched a finger to his lips. "You'd better not be lying, Norman. I'll leave you if I ever find you with someone else."

"You won't," he said. "You're the only girl for me, Bessie." He wrapped his arms around her and pulled her close. But over her shoulder he stared unhappily at the curtain hiding his clothes.

Elsie had stitched it for him the first time she came to the farm.

He cleaned the hut to remove all trace of Bessie. Strands of blond hair. The smell of her perfume. One of her combs. He rescued the dirty sheets from the nesting box, then had to wash them to remove the smell of chickens. They ended up a uniform grey but gave no other clues that they'd been off the bed for seven weeks.

The tidiness of the shack was the first thing Elsie noticed. "Did you do this for me?" she asked. She looked pleased.

"I wanted it to look nice for you, Else. It was a bit mucky the last time you came."

"It didn't matter. I know how hard you have to work, lovey. I'll keep it spick and span when I'm living here all the time."

He changed the subject abruptly. "How are your parents?"

"The same." She frowned. "Mrs. Cosham said she was surprised to see me. That's a bit strange, don't you think? I booked the room ages ago."

Norman turned away to put the kettle on the stove.

"She asked me if we were still engaged. Why would she say that, pet?"

He gave an attempt at a shrug. "I don't know. Maybe she's wondering why you haven't been down so much this year."

"Did you tell her about my nerves? Does she know I'm on tablets?"

"No."

She sank on to the bed. "That's good. I'm not going to take them any more. I hate feeling drowsy all the time."

"But if they're making you better—"

"It's *you* that makes me better, Norman. Do you remember last summer? It was all so perfect. Just you and me in our own little house."

"That was the year before," he told her. "Last year was when you got the sack . . . and your brother and sister were married."

"We made love all the time, pet. You can't have forgotten."

"It was only kissing and cuddling. It's not as if we had sex."

She stared at him. "We *did* have sex, Norman. You nearly got me pregnant."

Norman frowned at her. "A bloke can't *nearly* get a girl pregnant, Else. Either he does or he doesn't. In any case, we never came close to making babies. You refused to do it until after the wedding."

"That's not true."

He shrugged. "You thought if I wanted sex that badly I'd marry you just to get it."

She looked confused suddenly. "You're lying."

"You know I'm not," he told her. "I don't say I wouldn't have liked it, but—" Another shrug as he moved towards the door. "The best summer was before we were engaged. You were pretty happy then. Do you want to make the tea? I've things to do outside."

Elsie took all the wrong messages from Norman's efforts to keep her out of sight. She thought it was eagerness that made him collect her from the Coshams before the sun came up. And passion that kept her in the shack until well after dark. Even his sudden use of "pet," "lovey" and "sweetheart" didn't rouse her suspicions.

"We can't go into town today, pet . . ." "Stay inside, lovey. I can't bear to think of you getting your hands dirty . . ." "It's a real holiday having you cook for me, sweetheart . . ."

Norman knew he was being cruel but he blamed Elsie for it. If she'd been halfway normal, he wouldn't have fallen out of love with her. She should have taken his hints and left long ago. How was a chap supposed to behave when he'd made a promise that he didn't want to keep?

With any other girl he could have said: "It hasn't worked . . . No hard feelings . . . Let's go our separate ways . . ."

With Elsie it would turn into the world's greatest drama. "You've broken my heart . . . I'm going to kill my-self . . . I want to die . . ."

The idea had formed in his mind that the easiest way to be shot of Elsie was to marry Bessie. Once he was wed, Elsie would have to leave him alone. His plan was to write her a letter the day after the wedding.

Dear Elsie,

    Yesterday I married a girl called Bessie Coldicott. She is now Mrs. Thorne. I'm sorry to break it to you like this but I knew you'd create a scene if I told you before.

    Yours, Norman

It was the coward's way out, but it was also the safest. If the letter made her unhappy, then her parents could jolly her out of it. And if they failed, then Norman would rather she killed herself in London than in Blackness Road.

"You do love me, don't you, pet?" Elsie pleaded on her last day at the farm.

"Of course."

"Then show me."

Norman watched with loathing as she undid her dress and let it slip from her shoulders. She was so thin that every rib stood out beneath her skin. In a pathetic attempt to make herself more appealing she took off her glasses and peered at him from eyes that couldn't see.

"Touch my breasts, pet." She used her hands to push her flat chest into a cleavage. "Are they pretty? Do you like them?" She dropped her right hand to her crotch. "Do you like this, Norman? Is *this* nice?"

Oh, God!

Tears wet Elsie's lashes. "Love me, pet. *Please*. I can't live without you. I'm so . . . *lonely*."

With a sense of shame, Norman pulled her to him. But all he could think of was Bessie . . .

> 86 Clifford Gardens
> Kensal Rise
> London

November 16th, 1924

My dearest beloved,

The most wonderful thing! Your little Elsie is pregnant. I missed a bleed this month and the doctor says I'm expecting. It must have been when you made love to me on my last day in the shack.

I know you didn't want a baby, pet, but I <u>promise</u> we can manage. It means we'll have to get married as soon as possible. Dad wants it to be before Christmas. He'd rather not walk me up the aisle if I'm showing.

Oh, my darling, I am so happy. Please say you're happy too and let me know how quickly you can arrange our wedding.

Your own loving wife,

Elsie xxx xxx

Blackness Road
Crowborough
Sussex

November 18th, 1924

Dear Elsie,

Your letter shocked me. How can you be pregnant when we've never had sex? There was <u>no</u> love-making at the shack. I hugged you when you said you were lonely, but I never took my clothes off. You <u>can't</u> be expecting a baby. The doctor's wrong.

Tell your dad you've invented this story to make me marry you. If you really are pregnant then it must be some other man's baby.

Yours,

Norman

86 Clifford Gardens
Kensal Rise
London

November 20th, 1924

My own darling Norman,

I know you're upset, and I'm sorry to bring this trouble on you. But it's no good putting your head in the sand. The doctor says a girl can get pregnant from heavy petting, and you know we've done that many times. We must make the best of this, lovey, and not get cross with each other.

Dad wants us to meet so that I can prove I'm not fibbing. He says it should be in a public place so that you won't be able to shout at me. Do you remember the tea shop at Groombridge? I shall wait for you there at 3 o'clock next Monday (24th). If you don't come, Dad says he will talk to your father in the evening. The baby is making me feel sick every morning, pet, and my condition will soon be obvious to everybody. I hope you love your little Elsie enough to do the right thing by her.

Your sweetheart,

Elsie xxx xxx

Chapter Seven

Groombridge—Monday, November 24th, 1924

The tea shop was a gloomy place. Thick lace curtains hung at the windows and dark panels lined the walls. Norman had taken Elsie there during the first summer at the farm. He'd perched her on his bicycle crosspiece and ridden the five miles to Groombridge. They'd snatched kisses as they rode through the Sussex countryside. Elsie had loved it even though her bottom had hurt for days afterwards.

Norman arrived early for the meeting but Elsie was already there. He spotted her immediately. She sat at a table in the corner, biting her nails and looking nervous. He wondered how long she'd been waiting. Hours probably. He guessed she'd been practising what to say since she wrote her letter.

She gave a little wave when she saw him. Then dropped her hand when he scowled at her. What was the point of talking to her? Did she really think he was stupid enough to accept a baby that didn't—*couldn't*—exist?

"I knew you'd come," she said as he pulled out the chair opposite her.

"You didn't give me much choice. I don't want my father dragged into your lies."

"I'm not lying." She put a protective hand on her belly. "I'm carrying your son, Norman."

Despite himself, his eyes were drawn to what she was guarding. "You're making it up, Elsie."

"That's not what the doctor says."

"How can he know? You were barely two weeks gone when you saw him. Assuming you ever went *near* a doctor. I don't believe that any more than this story you've made up about a baby."

Elsie smiled brightly as a waitress approached the table. "We'd like a pot of tea and some scones. My husband says I must eat for two now."

The woman laughed. "I'm pleased for you," she told Norman. "When's it due?"

"I don't know," he said, staring at Elsie. "When's it due, Else?"

"Next summer of course. You can't have forgotten already." She raised her eyes to the ceiling as if to say "Men!"

"Enjoy yourselves while you can is my advice," the waitress said, writing their order on her pad. "Life's never the same afterwards." She moved away to another table.

"You're off your rocker if you think I'm going to marry you without proof," said Norman in a low voice. "What do you think I'm going to do when this baby never arrives? Laugh? I'll be flaming mad."

Elsie kept the false, bright smile on her face. "Of course the baby's going to arrive. Mum says it's a boy because he's giving me awful morning sickness. She had the same trouble with my brother."

She tried to take one of Norman's hands but he pulled away from her.

"You might comfort me," she said. "It's frightening to find yourself pregnant when you don't have a husband."

"You're not pregnant, Elsie."

A glint of temper showed in her eyes. "Don't keep saying that."

"It's the truth."

"No, it's not," she hissed. "The truth is you did something you wish you hadn't . . . but it's too late, Norman. Now you have to marry me whether you like it or not." She rubbed her belly. "Unless you want your son to be born a bastard."

He didn't. He wanted a son he could be proud of. With Bessie. But he hesitated in the face of Elsie's anger.

"I don't see how you can be in the family way," he said lamely. "It doesn't make sense. How did it happen?"

This was the question she'd been waiting for. She launched into a hushed torrent of words, urging him to believe her. The doctor had told her that petting was far more dangerous than anyone realized. More babies were made by accident than were ever planned. A girl just had to touch a man and his sperm could find its way into her.

Norman shook his head in disbelief. "How?"

"If she puts her hand on herself afterwards. Here—" She pointed towards her crotch.

Was that true?

"I undid your buttons," she said. "That's when it must have happened." She lowered her voice to a sly whisper. "I was naked, remember."

Norman clenched his fists between his knees and stared at the table. Despite the sex he'd had with Bessie, his only real knowledge of the birth process was egg-hatching. "It can't be that easy, Else. Satan has to do the full thing."

"He's a chicken, pet. Humans are different."

Were they?

He wished he could ask Bessie. Even his father. As the waitress brought their tea and scones, he listened to Elsie prattle on about how they'd be a proper family by next summer. But her tone had a fake jollity, as if she was more intent on convincing strangers than convincing Norman.

Later, when he walked her to the station, she ordered him to arrange the wedding as soon as possible. "I'll tell Mum and Dad it'll happen before Christmas."

He refused her offer of a kiss. "You're taking a lot for granted, Elsie."

"Why shouldn't I?" she said with a tremor of fear in her voice. "It's *your* baby, Norman. You *have* to marry me."

"And if I don't?"

"I'll kill myself," she sobbed tearfully. "And you'll be to blame."

When Bessie came to the shack that evening Norman asked her if a girl could get pregnant by touching a man's "thing" when he had his clothes on. She giggled. "You mean like this?" she asked, feeling his penis through his trousers.

"No. Putting her hand through his fly . . . then touching her fanny afterwards."

"Like this?" She undid his buttons and fluttered her fingers around his foreskin before reaching under her skirt.

He grabbed her round the waist and nuzzled her neck. "I met a bloke this morning who said that's how his sister got pregnant."

"He's lying," said Bessie with another giggle. "The silly cow's been at it hammer and tongs and doesn't want her parents to know."

"That's what I thought."

"So who is this bloke?"

"No one you know," he said, lowering her on to the bed. "And I wouldn't tell you anyway. If the girl wants to lie that's her business."

"Except you'd have to be daft as a brush to believe rubbish like that. If touching was all it took . . . every girl in the world would be pregnant."

Blackness Road
Crowborough
Sussex

November 25th, 1924

Dear Elsie,

I have thought long and hard about what you said yesterday and I'm afraid I do not believe you're pregnant. For this reason, I shall not be arranging our wedding this week. There are one or two things I haven't told you. Life has been difficult this last year. The farm is in debt, and someone else has been helping me through my problems. I am between two fires at the moment and need time to decide what is best to do.

Yours,

Norman

86 Clifford Gardens
Kensal Rise
London

November 26th, 1924

My own darling Norman,

I don't understand. Of course I'm pregnant. Why won't you believe me? And who is this someone else? I really do think you owe me an explanation.

Your loving,

Elsie xxx

Blackness Road
Crowborough
Sussex

November 27th, 1924

Dear Elsie,

What I haven't told you is that a girl comes here late at night. It started when you gave in to your nerves again and felt that life wasn't worth living. I lost hope that we could ever be happy together. This other girl is different. She makes me laugh and keeps me going through the bad patches. I have strong feelings for her or I wouldn't have done what I've done.

I'm sorry to upset you.

Yours,

Norman

Blackness Road
Crowborough
Sussex

November 27th, 1924

Dear Dad,

I could do with some advice. I've run into some problems with the farm and with Elsie. Is there any chance you could visit in the next few days?

I'm sorry to be a nuisance.

Your loving son,

Norman

86 Clifford Gardens
Kensal Rise
London

November 28th, 1924

Dear Norman,

You've broken my heart. I never thought you could lie to me like this. I gave you myself and all my love and you have betrayed me. It's a poor thing for a man to give up on his wife just because her nerves are bad. You don't seem to care how I feel. You don't write a single word of love, yet I stood by you when you were out of work.

I expect you to finish with this other girl and marry me. Let me know what date you've fixed by return. I shall love you forever and always in spite of what you've done.

Your devoted,

Elsie xxx

CHAPTER EIGHT

Blackness Road—Sunday, November 30th, 1924

Norman jumped out of his skin when Elsie smacked him on the arm. He was busy cleaning out the chicken sheds and had his back to the road. He was humming to himself and his mind was full of Bessie.

"What the hell—" he cried, ducking away from her and raising his arms to protect himself. He certainly hadn't expected to see Elsie.

She pounded at him with her fists. "I *hate* you," she spat. "Who's this other girl? What's her name? Why didn't you answer my letter?"

Norman warded off the blows. He'd never seen her so mad looking. Her hair was unkempt and her face red with anger. "I only got your letter this morning," he fibbed.

"Liar! You'd have got it yesterday. I want my wedding, Norman. When's it going to be?" She kicked his leg. "*Tell me!*" she screamed.

Chickens scattered in alarm. "Take it easy," he begged. "You're scaring the hens."

But she wouldn't be side-tracked. "*Now*, Norman . . . tell me *now*."

"Soon," he said desperately, dodging another punch. "It'll be soon."

She dropped her fists. "When?"

"Before Christmas."

She examined his face to see if he was lying. "That had better be the truth. If I find out you're lying again—" She broke off on a sob. "How *could* you, pet? I thought I could trust you."

"You can," he said lamely. "I was planning to write today. Do your parents know you're here?"

She shook her head.

"Then they'll be worried. You should go home. I'll walk you to the station."

"I'm not leaving," she said stubbornly. "I won't go back to London till I'm a married woman. Everyone's saying it's never going to happen. But it *is*. You're promised to me . . . you've *always* been promised to me."

What could Norman say other than yes? There was no reasoning with Elsie when she was like this. He wanted to tell her to take a tablet but feared another onslaught from her fists. In this mood, anything could fuel her anger. And he had a bigger problem. He needed to be rid of her before Bessie came to the shack that evening.

So he lied. He told Elsie he loved her. That he wanted her baby. That of course the wedding was on. The other girl was history. Just a silly mistake that had happened when he was lonely.

"But you must go home now, Else. You can't stay here till we're married. People will talk."

"I don't care."

"But *I* do," he said firmly, steering her towards the gate. "I want a wife I can be proud of . . . not one that's called a tart."

And of course Elsie gave in. As Norman knew she would. It was her worst fear. That people would sneer at her behind her back.

But did anyone—apart from Norman and her family —even remember that Elsie Cameron existed?

That night Norman told Bessie the truth. He did it badly. Kept starting with: "Do you remember when I said . . ."

Bessie took it in her stride. "I'm not an idiot, Norman. I found Elsie's love letters weeks ago. That's what women do . . . search their men's things."

He was more relieved than offended. "And?"

"I asked Mrs. Cosham about her. She said Elsie's got mental problems . . . and you're the poor lad who drew the short straw. Elsie couldn't care less who she marries, as long as she marries someone."

"I liked her at the beginning, Bess."

She propped her hip against his arm. "You were a baby . . . chickenfeed to the first grasping woman you met. You have to be straight with her. Tell her you don't love her any more."

"It's not that easy. She gets"—he sought for a word —"hysterical." He sighed. "I wish she'd just go away and leave me alone."

"But types like that don't, Norm. She'll keep at you till you do what she wants. I knew a bloke like it once. Walked out with him a couple of times and he acted as if he owned me. Even smacked me in the face once because he reckoned I was smiling at another man."

Norman was shocked. It was one thing for Elsie to hit him, another for a man to do it to Bessie. "What happened?"

"My dad sorted him out. Told him he'd take his head off his shoulders if he came near me again. It worked a treat. He left town and I never saw him again. Maybe you should ask your father to do the same for you."

"Dad's never hit a woman in his life."

"He doesn't need to. All he has to do is make Elsie understand that you're never going to marry her. She might believe it if it comes from him."

But Mr. Thorne refused to do his son's dirty work. It was three days later when he came to the farm in response to Norman's letter. They were inside the shack, sheltering from the wind. Norman stuttered through another explanation, then asked his father to speak to Elsie on his behalf.

Mr. Thorne cast a critical eye over his son's living arrangements. "You can't bring a wife into this," he said.

"I know . . . but Elsie won't listen to me, Dad. She might to you, though."

"Maybe she will, but it's a shabby way to tell her you're not going to marry her. I thought I brought you up to be more honest than that, son."

"You did, but—"

"I'm disappointed in you, Norman. You're a Methodist with Christian values. You should never have invited her here on her own."

"I know, but—"

"I thought you had more sense."

"But I never *did* anything, Dad."

"Are you sure?"

"Positive. It might have happened the way she says the first summer we were here. We got pretty close at times." He squeezed one fist inside the other. "She's lying. I'll eat my hat if she's even been to a doctor."

Mr. Thorne sighed. "Then don't commit yourself to a wedding until well after Christmas. If she's telling the truth, it should be obvious by the spring. If she isn't, you can be shot of her with a good conscience."

"But you don't know what she's like," Norman said wretchedly. "When she came here on Sunday, she was planning to stay until I married her. What if she tries that again?"

"Show her who's boss," Mr. Thorne said reasonably. "Give her her marching orders. Put her on the train."

Norman massaged his knuckles. "You've never seen her when she's angry. She's like a mad woman . . . screaming and yelling."

"I thought she was taking pills for her nerves."

"Not on Sunday, she wasn't. She kept hitting me."

Mr. Thorne frowned. "It's a bad business, son. But I did warn you."

Tears of despair rose in Norman's throat. "So what do I do?" he asked gruffly. "I don't even like her any more . . . and I sure as hell don't want to marry her."

"Then keep delaying. There's nothing else to be done. Except pray that you're right about her not being pregnant."

"I am right, Dad. I don't need to pray about it."

"Then *I* will," said Mr. Thorne, standing up. "I'm not as arrogant as you, Norman. It's God who decides when and how a child is born."

"Supposing Elsie *is* in the family way?" Norman asked Bessie that evening. "No one's going to believe it isn't mine. I'll have to marry her whether I like it or not."

"She's not."

"How do you know?"

"She can't even persuade you to sleep with her."

He rested his forehead in his hands. "She's not that ugly, Bess."

"All right. Let's say another man *has* shown an interest. Why would she want to marry you and not him?"

"Maybe he's married already."

Bessie gave a grunt of amusement. "Oh, come on! Where would they have done it? In her parents' bed? In his *wife's* bed?"

"That's disgusting."

"Well, her only other choice would have been a stand-up quickie in a back alley. Is she a prostitute?"

"Don't be stupid."

"It's you who's being stupid, Norman. There's no *way* Elsie can be pregnant. Your dad's right. You have to stick it out and call her bluff . . . even if she does make your life hell in the meantime . . ."

Blackness Road
Crowborough
Sussex

December 3rd, 1924

Dear Elsie,

Dad came to visit today. He's not happy about a rushed wedding and says we must wait till after Christmas. Hope you understand.

Yours,

Norman

CHAPTER NINE

Kensal Rise, north London—
Friday, December 5th, 1924

The hairdresser had pinned Elsie's hair into a neat coil at the back. Now she teased the fringe into a cloud of soft curls around the girl's face. "Going somewhere nice?" she asked, nodding towards the overnight case at Elsie's feet.

Elsie stared at herself in the mirror. She'd asked for a new style that took attention away from her glasses. Had it worked? Did it make her look pretty? "Sussex," she said.

"I went to Brighton once."

"I'm having my wedding there."

"That's nice," the woman said. "I suppose it's cheaper out of season. When's the big day?"

"Tomorrow."

"Goodness! Who's the lucky chap?"

"Norman Thorne," Elsie told her. "He's a farmer . . . has his own house and everything."

The woman smiled. "And all I got was two rooms and a dustman. Where did I go wrong, eh?" She framed Elsie's face with her hands. "How's that, dear? Will it suit?"

"Oh, yes. Norman won't recognise me." Elsie lifted the little case on to her lap and moved aside a wash bag to find her purse. "How much?"

"Sixpence should cover it."

The hairdresser couldn't help noticing how little was in the case. A baby's frock, two pairs of shoes and the wash bag. She wondered what kind of girl would go to her new home with no knickers.

There was even less in the purse. When Elsie had paid for her new hairdo, there were only a couple of pennies and a train ticket left. *Still* . . . It wasn't a hairdresser's place to question a client's word.

But, oh, my goodness! How she longed to tell the skinny little thing that her green knitted dress didn't suit her. And that chewed fingernails and the desperation behind her horn-rimmed glasses put lovers off quicker than anything.

Blackness Road
Crowborough
Sussex

Sunday, December 7th, 1924

My own darling Elsie,

Well, where did you get to yesterday? You said you were coming on Saturday so I went to the station to meet you. Did something go wrong? Let me know as soon as possible.

Your ever loving,

Norman

Telegram, 10.00 a.m. Wednesday, December 10th, 1924

From: Donald Cameron, 86 Clifford Road, Kensal Rise, London

To: Norman Thorne, Wesley Poultry Farm, Crowborough

Elsie left Friday. Have heard no news. Has she arrived? Reply.

Telegram, dated 3.00 p.m. Wednesday,
December 10th, 1924

From: Norman Thorne, Wesley Poultry Farm,
Crowborough

To: Donald Cameron, 86 Clifford Road,
Kensal Rise, London

Not here. Cannot understand. Sent letter on Sunday.

CHAPTER TEN

Blackness Road, Crowborough—
Friday, December 12th, 1924

It was at times like this that PC Beck wished he was thinner. It was hard work pedalling his heavy cycle along Blackness Road. When he reached the Wesley Poultry Farm and saw the muddy state of the field, he gave up on the bike and went looking for Mr. Thorne on foot.

He found him in one of the chicken sheds. "Mr. Thorne? *Norman* Thorne?"

"That's me." Norman wiped his palms down his trousers and offered an open hand. "Sorry about the mess. The rain's chewed up the ground. What can I do for you?"

The policeman returned the handshake. "I'm here about Miss Elsie Cameron, sir. I believe you and she are engaged."

"That's right. Has she had an accident or something?"

"That's what we're trying to find out. Her father reported her missing yesterday. He says she left London a week ago to come down here."

Norman shook his head. "I haven't seen her. She told me she was coming on Saturday . . . but she never turned up. I wrote the next day to ask what was going on but I haven't had a reply. All I've had is a telegram from her dad."

"Do you mind telling me what you were doing last Friday, Mr. Thorne?"

"Not in the least." Norman gestured towards his shed. "How about a cup of tea? It's warmer inside. I can give you a photograph of Elsie if it helps. I'm pretty damn worried about her, you know."

But not worried enough to come to the police station himself, thought PC Beck sourly as he picked his way through the mud. He studied the picture of Elsie while Norman set the kettle to boil.

"Mr. Cameron says she left his house on Friday afternoon," he said, taking out his notebook. "Do you want to give me your movements from lunchtime onwards?"

Norman's memory was surprisingly good. He recalled in great detail what he had been doing on Friday, December 5th. Shortly after lunch he had cycled to Tunbridge Wells to buy some shoes. On his return at around four o'clock he had fed his chickens and collected some milk from Mr. and Mrs. Cosham.

"After that I made some tea and took a nap," he said. "I was whacked. The round trip to Tunbridge Wells is a killer."

"But Miss Cameron didn't come here?"

"No. I went out again a bit later . . . about a quarter to ten I should think. I'd promised to walk a couple of lady friends home from the station. Mrs. Coldicott and her daughter. They spent the day in Brighton and came back on the ten o'clock train."

"Address?"

Norman gave it to him. "I stayed at their house about fifteen minutes and was back here for half-eleven. There was no sign of Elsie . . . but I wasn't expecting her till Saturday."

"How do you know the Coldicotts?"

"The way I know most people round here. Mrs. Coldicott buys a hen from time to time."

"What did you do on Saturday, Mr. Thorne?"

"Fed and watered the chickens then went to the station to meet Elsie. She told me she'd be coming in on the ten-fifteen. I waited around for an hour then caught the train to Tunbridge Wells."

"Was that normal?"

"What?"

"That she stood you up?"

Norman stared at him for a moment. "I didn't think of it as standing up. I assumed she'd had to stay home for some reason. Do you mean was I worried?"

"If you like."

"Why should I have been?"

PC Beck shrugged. "No reason. What did you do in Tunbridge Wells on Saturday?"

"Nothing much. Walked around a bit, then came home again. I checked at the station in case Elsie had come on a later train, but no one had seen her. So I stopped off at the Coshams for some milk and asked if she'd booked in with them. But she hadn't."

"Is that where she usually stayed?"

Norman nodded. "They'd planned a party for Saturday night. I was hoping to take Elsie to it."

"Did you go anyway?"

"No. The Coshams cancelled it because not enough people could come."

The policeman made a note. "What did you do instead?"

"Went to the Coldicott house. There was a film I wanted to see at the cinema. I asked Miss Coldicott if she wanted to come with me."

PC Beck took another glance at the photograph of Elsie. "How old is Miss Coldicott?"

"Twenty."

"Is she a special friend, Mr. Thorne?"

"No. She just likes going to the movies."

"And you say you wrote to Miss Cameron the next day, asking what had happened to her?"

"That's correct."

"Do you have her letter to you, saying she'd be down on Saturday?"

"We didn't arrange it by letter. She was here the weekend before. We agreed the day and time then."

PC Beck took the mug of tea that Norman handed to him. "Do you have any idea what might have happened to her?"

Norman shook his head again. "I did wonder if she nodded off on the train and ended up in Brighton. She takes pills for her nerves. They make her go to sleep in the oddest places."

"But she wouldn't have stayed there, would she?"

Norman pulled a face. "I don't know. She might be trying to scare us into taking notice of her. She can act pretty strange at times."

PC Beck gave a report of this conversation to his inspector.

"What did you make of him?" the man asked.

"He's a young chap. Looks as if he's struggling to make ends meet. His place is more like a pigsty than a chicken farm. But he's pleasant enough and looks you in the eye when he answers questions."

"So you think he's telling the truth?"

"I checked with Mr. and Mrs. Cosham and they confirmed what he said. I also visited the Coldicotts. They did the same. But I'm not sure Bessie Coldicott is quite the casual friend he claimed. She's a handsome piece and she talked about Thorne's farm as if she's a regular visitor."

"Interesting." The inspector steepled his fingers under his nose. "According to Mr. Cameron, his daughter was pregnant by Thorne. Is Bessie attractive enough to make the lad wish he hadn't been so careless?"

"Oh, yes," said Beck dryly. "In terms of looks, there's no contest."

Elsie's photograph appeared in the newspapers that weekend under the caption: "*Has anyone seen this woman?*"

It prompted two flower growers in Crowborough to come forward. They told the police they'd passed someone matching Elsie's description at ten past five on the day she went missing. She was walking in the direction of Wesley Poultry Farm.

This time a team of officers visited Norman's farm. He was asked if he had any objections to the huts being searched. "Of course not," he told them. "I want to help all I can."

The inspector sent his men to check the chicken sheds while he went into the shack with Norman. He refused to sit down or take a cup of tea. Instead he moved about the room, pulling open drawers and examining Norman's clothes.

He asked Norman the same questions that PC Beck had asked. And received the same answers. "You have a good memory, Mr. Thorne."

"My life's pretty boring. There's not much to remember."

"So the last time Elsie came here was Sunday, November 30th?"

Norman nodded. "I haven't seen her since."

The inspector eyed him for a moment. "And how often have you seen Miss Coldicott in that time?"

"Just once," said Norman truthfully.

Bessie had been in the shack when a reporter came to the door. Norman hid her from view by stepping outside and closing the door behind him. But Bessie had taken fright.

"I don't want to be in the papers," she said after the reporter had left. She was trembling.

Norman tried to comfort her.

"No," she said, pushing him away. "I can't see you again till this is over. I won't bring scandal on my family,

Norm." She slipped away in the dark without saying goodbye.

The inspector might have been reading Norman's mind. "I'm told you've had reporters here, Mr. Thorne."

"I didn't invite them. They just keep coming."

"But you show them around and let them take photographs of you with your chickens."

Norman gave a morose shrug. "What else can I do? If I refuse, they'll say I have something to hide. They hang around the gate, waiting for me to come out."

The inspector felt sorry for the lad. He had no liking for the press either. "It's not easy. What are these stains?" he asked, pointing to the table.

"Blood and guts," said Norman. "It's where I pluck and pull my hens. Sometimes I joint them and take their heads off. It depends what the customer wants. There's a fair amount of mess if I do a batch at a time."

"Where do you hang the birds?"

"From a beam in one of the empty sheds." He looked up. "Sometimes from this beam."

The inspector followed his gaze. "The one you keep your hats on?"

"Yes. I move them to make room."

"How do you reach it?"

"Stand on a chair."

"May I?"

Norman pushed a seat towards him. "Be my guest."

The inspector hoisted himself up and looked along the beam. "It's very clean. The upper beam's dusty . . . but not this one."

"It's harder to reach the top. If I stored anything up there, I wouldn't be able to get it down."

"But why are there are no feathers, Mr. Thorne? You seem to have done a splendid job of cleaning this place."

"I do my best. A chap shouldn't let his standards go just because he lives alone."

The inspector stepped down and replaced the chair under the table. "But you don't feel the same about the outside? Your chicken runs look as if you've taken a plough to them."

"It's the hens. They scratch for worms."

The lad had an answer for everything, the inspector thought. He watched Norman closely as he asked his next question. "Why was Elsie walking along Blackness Road the day she went missing, Mr. Thorne?"

Norman's eyes widened slightly. "I don't understand."

"Two witnesses saw her at five-ten. They said she was heading here."

"It can't have been Elsie."

"They recognised her from the photograph you gave us."

"Well, she never arrived," Norman said flatly. "I'll swear on any Bible you like that I have not seen Elsie Cameron since the end of November."

Blackness Road

December 31st

My darling Bessie,

It's been so long since I saw you. I really hoped we could spend Christmas together. But things are getting better now. The reporters have gone and the police accept that Elsie never came here. I now wonder if she killed herself in secret somewhere. She always said she'd do it if I let her down.

She had a strange nature and not very kind parents. They forced her on me because they were bored with her moods. I should have listened to my father. But like you say, I was too young to know what I was doing.

Honour bright, darling, I have never felt for any girl as I do for you. I was drawn to Elsie out of loneliness. I'm drawn to you out of love. Dearest of pals, you keep me going through the dark hours. I hope it won't be long before this nightmare is over and we can be together again.

Your own dear,

Norman

Groombridge Road
Crowborough

January 13th

Dear Norman,

Sorry not to have replied before but we've been busy at work. I don't think we should see each other for a while. Dad doesn't want me walking out with you until the police go away. People might gossip. I'll write again when I can. Mum and Dad aren't too keen, though.

With love,

Bessie

Chapter Eleven

Wesley Poultry Farm, Blackness Road—
January 14th, 1925

A shadow darkened the doorway of the shack. Norman looked up from Bessie's letter to see a stranger standing there. Hastily, he used the sleeve of his jumper to wipe tears from his eyes. "Can I help you?" he asked.

"Chief Inspector Gillan of Scotland Yard, Mr. Thorne. I'm here to arrest you."

"What for?"

"Involvement in the disappearance of Miss Elsie Cameron. We have a warrant to dig up your property."

Norman looked past him to where several policemen were leaning on spades. "What happened to the other inspector?"

"Scotland Yard was called in a week ago. I've been running the case since your neighbour, Mrs. Annie Price, gave evidence to Sussex police. She saw Miss Cameron walk through your gate at five-fifteen on the evening of December 5th."

Norman knew Annie Price. She was one of Bessie's despised curtain twitchers. A woman with nothing better to do in life than spy on her neighbours. "It wasn't Elsie," he said.

The Chief Inspector stepped into the shack. "Then who was it, Mr. Thorne?" He read Bessie's letter over Norman's shoulder. "Miss Coldicott?"

"It wasn't anyone. I was here alone."

Gillan put a hand under the young man's arm and hauled him to his feet. "I'm betting Elsie's somewhere in this ploughed field, Norman. But if I'm wrong, I'll be the first to say sorry."

Four hours later, Norman was asked to account for the contents of an Oxo-cube tin. Found under a pile of rubbish in his tool shed, the tin contained a broken wrist-watch, some cheap jewellery and a bracelet.

"Do these belong to Elsie Cameron?" Gillan asked him.

"Yes . . . but it's not what you think. She hid them there the last time she came."

"Why? They aren't worth anything."

The question threw Norman. "I don't know," he said. "She didn't tell me why."

At nine-thirty the next morning, Gillan showed him Elsie's overnight case. It was sodden and filthy. "Do you recognise any of this?" he asked, removing the baby's frock, the two pairs of shoes, the wash bag and a pair of damaged spectacles.

Norman stared at the items.

"The case was buried near your hut. We think these are Miss Cameron's glasses. Who put them there?"

Norman didn't answer.

"If we find her body, you'll be charged with murder. Do you understand that? And the penalty for murder is to be hanged by the neck until you're dead. Is there anything you want to tell me that might save your life?"

Norman ran his tongue across dry lips. "No," he whispered.

Ten hours later, he changed his mind. At eight o'clock in the evening he asked to speak to Chief Inspector Gillan.

"I didn't kill Elsie," he told him, "but I know where her body is. It's under the chicken run where the Leghorns are."

"Do you want to make a statement, Norman?"

"Yes."

"Then I must remind you that anything you say will be taken down and may be used in evidence against you."

Sussex Constabulary

Statement given by Norman Thorne at 8.15 p.m. on January 15th, 1925

I was surprised when Elsie arrived at the farm on Friday, 5 December. It was shortly after five o'clock in the evening. She was in an angry mood. She calmed down when I gave her a cup of tea and some bread and butter. I asked her why she had come and where she planned to sleep.

She said she was going to sleep in the shack. And that she intended staying there until we were married. I told her she couldn't do that and we had a bit of a row. At seven-thirty, I went to the Coshams to see if they could put her up for the night. They were out.

When I got back to the farm Elsie was in a bad temper. We had a row about Bessie Coldicott. Elsie cried because I'd been unfaithful. I cooked her a boiled egg to raise her spirits. She

97

calmed down again until about nine-thirty when I told her I had to meet Bessie off the train.

Elsie tried to stop me going. She yelled at me and pulled me towards the bed. She said she wanted me to sleep with her. I refused and told her to go to bed on her own. She started sobbing. I could hear her as I went to the gate.

I walked Bessie and her mother home from the station then returned to the farm about half past eleven. The light was on in the shack. It was shining through the window. When I opened the door I saw Elsie hanging from the beam by a piece of washing-line cord. I couldn't believe it. I cut the cord and laid her on the bed. She was dead. She had her frock off and her hair was down. I put out the light and lay on the table for about an hour.

I thought about going to Dr. Turle and knocking up someone to call the police. Then I realised the position I was in. There were so many people who knew I didn't want to marry Elsie. Who would believe I hadn't killed her? The only thing I could think to do was bury her body and pretend I'd never seen her.

I got out my hacksaw and sawed off her legs and head by the glow of the fire. I did that because I thought smaller pieces would be easier to bury. I put her head in a biscuit tin and wrapped the rest in newspaper. I dug holes in the chicken run nearest the gate and put Elsie into them.

Then I burnt her clothes and cleaned the shack. I was afraid to tell the truth before. Elsie always said she'd kill herself if I let her down. But I never thought she'd do it.

Signed:

Norman Thorne

Chapter Twelve

Crowborough police station—January 16th, 1925

Chief Inspector Gillan folded his hands on the table. "What happened to the washing-line cord?"

"I burnt it with her clothes."

"Why did you do that? Why did you keep her jewellery?"

Norman ground his knuckles into his eyes. "I moved all her things on to the bed when I cut her up . . . then forgot about them. She was completely naked . . . nothing on at all." He took a breath. "I found her stuff when I started to clean up . . . but I was too tired to dig any more holes by then. It was simpler to throw her clothes on the fire and hide her jewellery in the tool shed."

"You buried her suitcase."

"I didn't want to burn the baby's dress. It didn't seem right."

Gillan offered him a cigarette. "The post-mortem showed she wasn't pregnant. You were telling the truth about that at least."

"I know."

"But you're lying about everything else, Norman. She didn't hang herself. There were no rope marks on her neck. And there's no sign that a body ever swung from your beams. They're made of soft pine. There should be a groove where the cord bit into the wood."

"I can only tell you what I found."

"Then explain how her watch and glasses came to be broken."

"Maybe she broke them herself. She was very het up."

"Not good enough."

"Maybe I broke them when I lay on the table. Maybe she stood on them after she took them off." Norman dropped his head into his hands. "She was blind as a bat . . . but she thought she looked better without them."

"Did she?"

"No."

Gillan ran his finger down a piece of paper in front of him. "The body was in good condition because the weather was cold and you buried it the same night. The post-mortem found bruises on Elsie's face. Did you punch her?"

"Of course not. I never hit Elsie."

"You had an argument with her."

"But I didn't *hit* her, Mr. Gillan. I wouldn't have told you about the row if I had. She went down like a sack of potatoes when I cut the cord. I was standing on a chair, and there was no way I could support her weight. I think her head knocked against the chest of drawers. Would that have caused bruises?"

"I don't know. I'm not an expert." The Scotland Yard man moved his finger down a line. "According to this, she died two hours after eating a light meal."

Norman leaned forward eagerly. "Then that proves I didn't kill her. She was alive when I left the shack at nine-thirty."

"There's only your word for that."

"Except we didn't have supper till after eight-thirty. First, I went to the Coshams and then we had a row about Bessie before I started cooking."

"But there are no witnesses to any of this, Norman. The Coshams were out and you and Elsie were alone."

"How would I know the Coshams were out if I didn't go there?"

Gillan shrugged. "It was a month before you made your statement. Anyone could have told you."

Norman wiped his palms nervously down his trousers. "But if she didn't hang herself . . . and I didn't hit her . . . then how does the post-mortem say I killed her?"

Gillan took his time about replying. This was the one bit that troubled him. "It says she died from shock."

"What does that mean?"

"Her nervous system failed. Her heart stopped and she collapsed."

Norman stared at him. "Does that mean her nerves killed her? How could that happen? She was always giving in to them . . . but she never came close to dying before."

"It depends what you did to her. This report suggests you punched her several times in the face then left her to die. If you hadn't . . . if you'd stayed with her and brought her some help . . . then I wouldn't be charging you with murder."

"But I didn't do anything, Mr. Gillan. You have to believe that. It happened the way I said in my statement."

Gillan pushed back his chair. "Then you shouldn't have taken her head off. It's easier to see rope marks when the neck's intact." He stood up. "You treated that poor girl with no more respect than you show a dead chicken. And policemen don't like that, Norman."

CHAPTER THIRTEEN

His Majesty's Prison, Lewes—March 3rd, 1925

As Norman's trial approached three months later, his defence team became worried about his state of mind. He was putting his faith in God and seemed unaware that the weight of the evidence was against him. Sir Bernard Spilsbury, England's most famous pathologist, had carried out the post-mortem. And Spilsbury had come down firmly in favour of murder.

The chief medical expert for the defence was Dr. Robert Brontë. He had performed a second post-mortem and was willing to say he'd found rope marks on Elsie's neck. He would also argue that "death by shock" should not result in a murder conviction. There was no evidence that Elsie's death was intended. Nor that a collapse could have been predicted.

But Dr. Brontë enjoyed none of Spilsbury's fame and the jury was less likely to believe him. Spilsbury had been the crown expert witness on every famous murder trial since 1910. His word alone could swing a jury.

The defence team felt that only Norman's father could make him understand how serious his position was. To this end, Mr. Thorne was given leave to speak to his son in Lewes Prison the day before the trial. He was shown to a room on the ground floor of the remand wing.

"Bearing up all right?" he asked when Norman was brought in.

They shook hands. "Pretty much. It's good to see you, Dad."

He looked so young, thought Mr. Thorne. Just a boy still. "Sit down, son. Your barrister, Mr. Cassels, has asked me to talk to you about the trial. We're all praying for a not guilty verdict, but—" He broke off. How could he tell his only child that he might hang?

Norman reached across the table and gently stroked his father's hand. "But the jury might believe this Spilsbury fellow?"

Mr. Thorne nodded.

"Mr. Cassels says they have to prove I *meant* to kill Elsie. But how can they do that if she died of shock? You can't *frighten* someone to death."

"Spilsbury will argue that the bruises on her face show you hit her . . . and that her watch and glasses were broken during the attack. If she was in a bad way when you left her to meet Bessie, then the jury might feel you meant her to die."

"What about the rope marks that Dr. Brontë found?"

Mr. Thorne sighed. "It's only his opinion, Norman. Spilsbury will say there were no rope marks."

"But there *were*, Dad. I saw them when I cut the cord away from Elsie's neck. I just don't understand why they can't tell she died from hanging. Doesn't it show in your lungs if you can't breathe?"

"She may never have intended to kill herself. According to Dr. Brontë, just drawing a noose round your neck can cause shock."

"That's what Mr. Cassels said. But I don't understand why."

"It's something called the vagal reflex. Some people are extremely sensitive to pressure on their necks. There's a case of a woman who died within three seconds of her lover's hand caressing her throat."

"But I found Elsie hanging, Dad. She *meant* to do it."

"Perhaps not. Perhaps it was a little piece of drama that went wrong."

Norman shook his head. "I still don't understand."

"Dr. Brontë thinks she was planning to frighten you. If she had the noose ready for when you came home . . . then stood on the chair when she heard the gate open—" Mr. Thorne broke off on another sigh. "Death by vagal reflex would have caused her to fall forward. That's why you found her hanging."

Norman stared. "Are you saying it was an accident?"

His father nodded. "It could have been. Which is why there were no marks on the beam. She wasn't there long enough. Not if you cut her down as soon as you found her."

"I did," Norman said with sudden excitement.

"Will the jury believe me? Will they believe Dr. Brontë?"

"Maybe . . . if we can prove she used threats of suicide to get her own way. We can certainly prove she was no stranger to play-acting. She told everyone she was pregnant. Even bought a baby's dress to keep up the pretence."

"I *told* you she was lying, Dad. Her parents should have put her in a hospital. She wasn't right in the head. She needed help."

"Two of her co-workers will say that in court, but whether anyone will believe them—" Mr. Thorne lapsed into a brief silence. "You should have gone to the police when you found her, Norman. Why didn't you?"

His son's eyes grew bleak. "Because they wouldn't have believed me. They don't believe me now."

"They might have done. It was cutting her up that makes people think you're a murderer. Elsie deserved better, Norman."

A shudder ran through the boy's frame.

"What made you do it?"

Tears wet Norman's lashes. "It didn't seem so bad. She was just another dead thing. I reckon you shut down your feelings when you have to kill chickens all the time. Will the jury understand that, Dad?"

"No, son," said Mr. Thorne sadly. "I don't think they will."

EPILOGUE

Norman Thorne was found guilty of the murder of Elsie Cameron on March 16th, 1925. He was sentenced to death by hanging. The date of his execution was fixed for April 22nd. By strange chance, this would have been Elsie's twenty-seventh birthday had she lived.

Public concern was expressed about the verdict. There were many who felt the trial had failed to prove "beyond reasonable doubt" that Norman had caused, or meant to cause, Elsie's death. Even Sir Arthur Conan Doyle—the creator of Sherlock Holmes—was moved to ask questions.

It came to nothing. Norman's appeal against his conviction and sentence was rejected. The night before his hanging, he wrote to his father. It was a letter full of hope.

> There will be a flash and all will be finished. No, not finished, just starting for I go to God. I'll wait for you just as others are waiting for me. I am free from sin. With all my love . . .

AUTHOR'S NOTE

It interests me that Norman Thorne never confessed to killing Elsie Cameron. Not even on the gallows. To the end, he swore he found her hanging in his shack. This doesn't prove he was innocent. But for a young man who believed in God, it was a dangerous gamble to take if he was guilty. Norman knew that a sinner must repent if he wanted to go to heaven.

I believe the truth is what I've suggested in this story. Elsie planned to frighten Norman when he came home by standing on a chair with a noose round her neck. But her cry for attention went wrong. Perhaps the cold made her clumsy. Perhaps she pulled the noose too tight by accident.

In some people, the vagal or carotid reflex kills rapidly. Compressing the nerves and arteries in the neck causes the brain to shut down and the heart to stop. This form of "accidental" death can occur during solo sex acts when a noose is used to enhance orgasm. Victims—usually men—tend to be recorded as "suicides" to avoid upsetting their families. However, the best-known use of reflex blackout is when Mr Spock presses his fingers to a person's neck in *Star Trek*. Even though *Star Trek* is fictional, the principle is the same.

Psychoanalysis was still in its infancy in 1924, but those who knew Elsie Cameron described her as mentally unstable. They said she was "depressed," "neurotic" and "nervy." She had a fear of being left on the shelf and thought people laughed at her. Her co-workers complained that she was "moody" and "difficult."

Her problems grew during her four-year relationship with Norman. She couldn't hold down a job. She wanted to be loved in a "fairy tale" way and was obsessed with getting married. She swung between anger and depression when she couldn't have her own way. A doctor tried to cure her condition with sedatives (probably an early form of barbiturates).

Elsie's behaviour suggests she suffered from Borderline Personality Disorder. Sufferers of BPD have low self-image and are often depressed. They can be difficult to live with. They have constant mood swings and become angry when they feel let down. They think in black-and-white terms, and form intense, conflict-ridden relationships. Threats of suicide are common.

Whatever happened the night Elsie died, I am sure her disturbed state of mind played a part in her death. Either her stubborn refusal to leave provoked Norman into hitting her, or she staged a "suicide" to make him feel guilty enough to give up Bessie.

At Norman's trial, the jury was swayed by Sir Bernard Spilsbury's testimony. They decided that Elsie collapsed as the result of an attack and that Norman had intended to kill her. Yet, even if he *had* hit her, there was no evidence she was dead when he left the shack. Nor that he could have predicted she would die later from shock.

I'm more persuaded by a sentence in Norman's statement. He said he found Elsie suspended from the beam with her "frock off and her hair down." Yet it was a cold December night. Norman himself would have been wearing an overcoat. Why would it even occur to him to say he found Elsie hanging naked . . .

. . . unless it was true?

THE TINDER BOX

***The Daily Telegraph—
Wednesday, 24th June, 1998

Sowerbridge Man Arrested

Patrick O'Riordan, 35, an unemployed Irish labourer, was charged last night with the double murder of his neighbours Lavinia Fanshaw, 93, and her live-in nurse, Dorothy Jenkins, 67. The murders have angered the small community of Sowerbridge where O'Riordan and his parents have lived for fifteen years. The elderly victims were brutally battered to death after Dorothy Jenkins interrupted a robbery on Saturday night. "Whoever killed them is a monster," said a neighbour. "Lavinia was a frail old lady with Alzheimer's who never hurt a soul." Police warned residents to remain calm after a crowd gathered outside the O'Riordan home when news of the arrest became public. "Vigilante behaviour will not be tolerated," said a spokesman. O'Riordan denies the charges.

11:30 P.M.—*Monday, 8th March, 1999*

Even at half past eleven at night, the lead news story on local radio was still the opening day of Patrick O'Riordan's trial. Siobhan Lavenham, exhausted after a fourteen-hour stint at work, listened to it in the darkness of her car while she negotiated the narrow country lanes back to Sowerbridge village.

". . . O'Riordan smiled as the prosecution case unfolded . . . harrowing details of how ninety-three-year-old Lavinia Fanshaw and her live-in nurse were brutally bludgeoned to death before Mrs. Fanshaw's rings were ripped from her fingers . . . scratch marks and bruises on the defendant's face, probably caused by a fight with one of the women . . . a crime of greed triggered by O'Riordan's known resentment of Mrs. Fanshaw's wealth . . . unable to account for his whereabouts at the time of the murders . . . items of jewellery recovered from the O'Riordan family home which the thirty-five-year-old Irishman still shares with his elderly parents . . ."

With a sinking heart, Siobhan punched the Off button and concentrated on her driving. "The Irishman . . ."

Was that a deliberate attempt to inflame racist division, she wondered, or just careless shorthand? God, how she loathed journalists! Confident of a guilty verdict, they had descended on Sowerbridge like a plague of locusts the previous week in order to prepare their background features in advance. They had found dirt in abundance, of course. Sowerbridge had fallen over itself to feed them with hate stories against the whole O'Riordan family.

She thought back to the day of Patrick's arrest, when Bridey had begged her not to abandon them. "You're one of us, Siobhan. Irish through and through, never mind you're married to an Englishman. You know my Patrick. He wouldn't hurt a fly. Is it likely he'd beat Mrs. Fanshaw to death when he's never raised a hand against his own father? Liam was a devil when he still had the use of his arm. Many's the time he thrashed Patrick with a stick when the drunken rages were on him, but never once did Patrick take the stick to him."

It was a frightening thing to be reminded of the bonds that tied people together, Siobhan had thought as she looked out of Bridey's window towards the silent, angry crowd that was gathering in the road. Was being Irish enough of a reason to side with a man suspected of slaughtering a frail bedridden old woman and the woman who looked after her?

"Patrick admits he stole from Lavinia," Siobhan had pointed out.

Tears rolled down Bridey's furrowed cheeks. "But not her rings," she said. "Just cheap trinkets that he was too ignorant to recognise as worthless paste."

"It was still theft."

"Mother of God, do you think I don't know that?" She held out her hands beseechingly. "A thief he may be, Siobhan, but never a murderer."

And Siobhan had believed her because she wanted to. For all his sins, she had never thought of Patrick as an aggressive or malicious man—too relaxed by half, many would say—and he could always make her and her children laugh with his stories about Ireland, particularly ones involving leprechauns and pots of gold hidden at the ends of rainbows. The thought of him taking a hammer to anyone was anathema to her.

And yet . . . ?

In the darkness of the car she recalled the interview she'd had the previous month with a detective inspector at Hampshire Constabulary Headquarters who seemed perplexed that a well-to-do young woman should have sought him out to complain about police indifference to the plight of the O'Riordans. She wondered now why she hadn't gone to him sooner.

Had she really been so unwilling to learn the truth . . . ?

Wednesday, 10th February, 1999

The detective shook his head. "I don't understand what you're talking about, Mrs. Lavenham."

Siobhan gave an angry sigh. "Oh, for goodness' sake! The hate campaign that's being waged against them. The graffiti on their walls, the constant telephone calls threatening them with arson, the fact that Bridey's too frightened to go out for fear of being attacked. There's a war going on in Sowerbridge which is getting worse the closer we come to Patrick's trial, but as far as you're concerned, it doesn't exist. Why aren't you investigating it? Why don't you respond to Bridey's telephone calls?"

He consulted a piece of paper on his desk. "Mrs. O'Riordan's made fifty-three emergency calls in the eight months since Patrick was remanded for the murders," he said, "only thirty of which were considered serious enough to send a police car to investigate. In every case, the attending officers filed reports saying Bridey was wasting police time." He gave an apologetic shrug. "I realise it's not what you want to hear, but we'd be within our rights if we decided to prosecute her. Wasting police time is a serious offence."

Siobhan thought of the tiny, wheelchair-bound woman whose terror was so real she trembled constantly. "They're after killing us, Siobhan," she would say over and over again. "I hear them creeping about the garden in the middle of the night and I think to myself, there's nothing me or Liam can do if this is the night they decide to break in. To be sure, it's only God who's keeping us safe."

"But who *are* they, Bridey?"

"It's the bully boys whipped up to hate us by Mrs. Haversley and Mr. Jardine," wept the woman. "Who else would it be?"

Siobhan brushed her long dark hair from her forehead and frowned at the detective inspector. "Bridey's old, she's disabled, and she's completely terrified. The phone never stops ringing. Mostly it's long silences, other times it's voices threatening to kill her. Liam's only answer to it all is to get paralytically drunk every night so he doesn't have to face up to what's going on." She shook her head impatiently. "Cynthia Haversley and Jeremy Jardine, who seem to control everything that happens in Sowerbridge, have effectively given carte blanche to the local youths to make life hell for them. Every sound, every shadow has Bridey on the edge of her seat. She needs protection, and I don't understand why you're not giving it to her."

"They were offered a safe house, Mrs. Lavenham, and they refused it."

"Because Liam's afraid of what will happen to Kilkenny Cottage if he leaves it empty," she protested. "The place will be trashed in half a minute flat. . . . You know that as well as I do."

He gave another shrug, this time more indifferent than apologetic. "I'm sorry," he said, "but there's nothing we can do. If any of these attacks actually happened . . . well, we'd have something concrete to investigate. They can't even name any of these so-called vigilantes . . . just claim they're yobs from neighbouring villages."

"So what are you saying?" she asked bitterly. "That they have to be dead before you take the threats against them seriously?"

"Of course not," he said, "but we do need to be persuaded the threats are real. As things stand, they seem to be all in her mind."

"Are you accusing Bridey of lying?"

He smiled slightly. "She's never been averse to embroidering the truth when it suits her purpose, Mrs. Lavenham."

Siobhan shook her head. "How can you say that? Have you ever spoken to her? Do you even *know* her? To you, she's just the mother of a thief and a murderer."

"That's neither fair nor true." He looked infinitely weary, like a defendant in a trial who has answered the same accusation in the same way a hundred times before. "I've known Bridey for years. It's part and parcel of being a policeman. When you question a man as often as I've questioned Liam, you get to know his wife pretty well by default." He leaned forward, resting his elbows on his knees and clasping his hands loosely in front of him. "And sadly, the one sure thing I know about Bridey is that you can't believe a word she says. It may not be her fault, but it *is* a fact. She's never had the courage to speak out honestly because her drunken brute of a husband beats her within an inch of her life if she even dares to think about it."

Siobhan found his directness shocking. "You're talking about things that happened a long time ago," she said. "Liam hasn't struck anyone since he lost the use of his right arm."

"Do you know how that happened?"

"In a car crash."

"Did Bridey tell you that?"

"Yes."

"Not so," he countered bluntly. "When Patrick was twenty, he tied Liam's arm to a table top and used a hammer to smash his wrist to a pulp. He was so wrought up that when his mother tried to stop him, he shoved her through a window and broke her pelvis so badly she's never been able to walk again. That's why she's in a wheelchair and why Liam has a useless right arm. Patrick got off lightly by pleading provocation because of Liam's past brutality towards him, and spent less than two years in prison for it."

Siobhan shook her head. "I don't believe you."

"It's true." He rubbed a tired hand around his face. "Trust me, Mrs. Lavenham."

"I can't," she said flatly. "You've never lived in Sowerbridge, Inspector. There's not a soul in that village who doesn't have it in for the O'Riordans and a juicy tidbit like that would have been repeated a thousand times. Trust *me*."

"No one knows about it." The man held her gaze for a moment, then dropped his eyes. "It was fifteen years ago and it happened in London. I was a raw recruit with the Met, and Liam was on our ten-most-wanted list. He was a scrap-metal merchant, and up to his neck in villainy, until Patrick scuppered him for good. He sold up when the lad went to prison and moved himself and Bridey down here to start a new life. When Patrick joined them after his release, the story of the car crash had already been accepted."

She shook her head again. "Patrick came over from Ireland after being wounded by a terrorist bomb. That's why he smiles all the time. The nerves in his cheek were severed by a piece of flying glass." She sighed. "It's another kind of disability. People take against him because they think he's laughing at them."

"No, ma'am, it was a revenge attack in prison for stealing from his cell mate. His face was slashed with a razor. As far as I know, he's never set foot in Ireland."

She didn't answer. Instead she ran her hand rhythmically over her skirt while she tried to collect her thoughts. *Oh, Bridey, Bridey, Bridey . . . Have you been lying to me . . . ?*

The inspector watched her with compassion. "Nothing happens in a vacuum, Mrs. Lavenham."

"Meaning what, exactly?"

"Meaning that Patrick murdered Mrs. Fanshaw"—he paused—"and both Liam and Bridey know he did. You can argue that the physical abuse he suffered at the hands of his father as a child provoked an anger in him that he couldn't control—it's a defence that worked after the attack on Liam— but it won't cut much ice with a jury when the victims were two defenceless old ladies. That's why Bridey's jumping at shadows. She knows that she effectively signed Mrs. Fanshaw's death warrant when she chose to keep quiet about how dangerous Patrick was, and she's terrified of it becoming public." He paused. "Which it certainly will during the trial."

Was he right? Siobhan wondered. Were Bridey's fears rooted in guilt? "That doesn't absolve the police of responsibility for their safety," she pointed out.

"No," he agreed, "except we don't believe their safety's in question. Frankly, all the evidence so far points to Liam himself being the instigator of the hate campaign.

The grafitti is always done at night in car spray paint, at least a hundred cans of which are stored in Liam's shed. There are never any witnesses to it, and by the time Bridey calls us the perpetrators are long gone. We've no idea if the phone rings as constantly as they claim, but on every occasion that a threat has been made, Bridey admits she was alone in the cottage. We think Liam is making the calls himself."

She shook her head in bewilderment. "Why would he do that?"

"To prejudice the trial?" he suggested. "He has a different mind-set from you and me, ma'am, and he's quite capable of trashing Kilkenny Cottage himself if he thinks it will win Patrick some sympathy with a jury."

Did she believe him? Was Liam that clever? "You said you were always questioning him. Why? What had he done?"

"Any scam involving cars. Theft. Forging M.O.T. certificates. Odometer fixing. You name it, Liam was involved in it. The scrap-metal business was just a front for a car-laundering operation."

"You're talking about when he was in London?"

"Yes."

She pondered for a moment. "Did he go to prison for it?"

"Once or twice. Most of the time he managed to avoid conviction. He had money in those days—a lot of money—and could pay top briefs to get him off. He shipped some of the cars down here, presumably with the intention of starting the same game again, but he was a broken man after Patrick smashed his arm. I'm told he gave up grafting for himself and took to living off disability benefit instead. There's no way anyone was going to employ him. He's too unreliable to hold down a job. Just like his son."

"I see," said Siobhan slowly.

He waited for her to go on, and when she didn't he said: "Leopards don't change their spots, Mrs. Lavenham. I wish I could say they did, but I've been a policeman too long to believe anything so naive."

She surprised him by laughing. "Leopards?" she echoed. "And there was me thinking we were talking about dogs."

"I don't follow."

"Give a dog a bad name and hang him. Did the police *ever* intend to let them wipe the slate clean and start again, Inspector?"

He smiled slightly. "We did . . . for fifteen years. . . . Then Patrick murdered Mrs. Fanshaw."

"Are you sure?"

"Oh, yes," he said. "He used the same hammer on her that he used on his father."

Siobhan remembered the sense of shock that had swept through the village the previous June when the two bodies were discovered by the local milkman after his curiosity had been piqued by the fact that the front door had been standing ajar at 5:30 on a Sunday morning. Thereafter, only the police and Lavinia's grandson had seen inside the house, but the rumour machine described a scene of carnage, with Lavinia's brains splattered across the walls of her bedroom and her nurse lying in a pool of blood in the kitchen. It was inconceivable that anyone in Sowerbridge could have done such a thing, and it was assumed the Manor House had been targeted by an outside gang for whatever valuables the old woman might possess.

It was never very clear why police suspicion had centred so rapidly on Patrick O'Riordan. Gossip said his fingerprints were all over the house and his toolbox was found in the kitchen, but Siobhan had always believed the police had received a tipoff. Whatever the reason, the matter appeared to be settled when a search warrant unearthed Lavinia's jewellery under his floorboards and Patrick was formally charged with the murders.

Predictably, shock had turned to fury but, with Patrick already in custody, it was Liam and Bridey who took the full brunt of Sowerbridge's wrath. Their presence in the village had never been a particularly welcome one—indeed, it was a mystery how "rough trade like them" could have afforded to buy a cottage in rural Hampshire, or why they had wanted to—but it became deeply unwelcome after the murders. Had it been possible to banish them behind a physical pale, the village would most certainly have done so; as it was, the old couple were left to exist in a social limbo where backs were turned and no one spoke to them.

In such a climate, Siobhan wondered, could Liam really have been stupid enough to ratchet up the hatred against them by daubing anti-Irish slogans across his front wall?

"If Patrick *is* the murderer, then why didn't you find Lavinia's diamond rings in Kilkenny Cottage?" she asked the inspector. "Why did you only find pieces of fake jewellery?"

"Who told you that? Bridey?"

"Yes."

He looked at her with a kind of compassion. "Then I'm afraid she was lying, Mrs. Lavenham. The diamond rings were in Kilkenny Cottage along with everything else."

2.

11:45 P.M.—Monday, 8th March, 1999

Siobhan was aware of the orange glow in the night sky ahead of her for some time before her tired brain began to question what it meant. Arc lights? A party? Fire, she thought in alarm as she approached the outskirts of Sower-bridge and saw sparks shooting into the air like a giant Roman candle. She slowed her Range Rover to a crawl as she approached the bend by the church, knowing it must be the O'Riordans' house, tempted to put the car into reverse and drive away, as if denial could alter what was happening. But she could see the flames licking up the front of Kilkenny Cottage by that time and knew it was too late for anything so simplistic. A police car was blocking the narrow road ahead, and with a sense of foreboding she obeyed the torch that signalled her to draw up on the grass verge beyond the church gate.

She lowered her window as the policeman came over, and felt the warmth from the fire fan her face like a Saharan wind. "Do you live in Sowerbridge, madam?" he asked. He was dressed in shirtsleeves, perspiration glistening on his forehead, and Siobhan was amazed that one small house two hundred yards away could generate so much heat on a cool March night.

"Yes." She gestured in the direction of the blaze. "At Fording Farm. It's another half-mile beyond the crossroads."

He shone his torch into her eyes for a moment—his curiosity whetted by her soft Dublin accent, she guessed—before lowering the beam to a map. "You'll waste a lot less time if you go back the way you came and make a detour," he advised her.

"I can't. Our driveway leads off the crossroads by Kilkenny Cottage and there's no other access to it." She touched a finger to the map. "There. Whichever way I go, I still need to come back to the crossroads."

Headlights swept across her rearview mirror as another car rounded the bend. "Wait there a moment, please." He moved away to signal towards the verge, leaving Siobhan to gaze through her windscreen at the scene of chaos ahead.

There seemed to be a lot of people milling around, but her night sight had been damaged by the brilliance of the flames; and the water glistening on the tarmac made it difficult to distinguish what was real from what was reflection. The rusted hulks of the old cars that littered the O'Riordans' property stood out in bold silhouettes against the light, and Siobhan thought that Cynthia Haversley had been right when she said they weren't just an eyesore but a fire hazard as well. Cynthia had talked dramatically about the dangers of petrol, but if there was any petrol left in the corroded tanks, it remained sluggishly inert. The real hazard was the time and effort it must have taken to manoeuvre the two fire engines close enough to weave the hoses through so many obstacles, and Siobhan wondered if the house had ever stood a chance of being saved.

She began to fret about her two small boys and their nanny, Rosheen, who were alone at the farmhouse, and drummed her fingers impatiently on the steering wheel. "What should I do?" she asked the policeman when he returned after persuading the other driver to make a detour. "I need to get home."

He looked at the map again. "There's a footpath running behind the church and the vicarage. If you're prepared to walk home, I suggest you park your car in the churchyard and take the footpath. I'll radio through to ask one of the constables on the other side of the crossroads to escort you into your driveway. Failing that, I'm afraid you'll have to stay here until the road's clear, and that could take several hours."

"I'll walk." She reached for the gear stick, then let her hand drop. "No one's been hurt, have they?"

"No. The occupants are away."

Siobhan nodded. Under the watchful eyes of half of Sowerbridge village, Liam and Bridey had set off that morning in their ancient Ford Estate, to the malignant sound of whistles and hisses. "The O'Riordans are staying in Winchester until the trial's over."

"So we've been told," said the policeman.

Siobhan watched him take a notebook from his breast pocket. "Then presumably you were expecting something like this? I mean, everyone knew the house would be empty."

He flicked to an empty page. "I'll need your name, madam."

"Siobhan Lavenham."

"And your registration number, please, Ms. Lavenham."

She gave it to him. "You didn't answer my question," she said unemphatically.

He raised his eyes to look at her but it was impossible to read their expression. "What question's that?"

She thought she detected a smile on his face and bridled immediately. "You don't find it at all suspicious that the house burns down the minute Liam's back is turned?"

He frowned. "You've lost me, Ms. Lavenham."

"It's *Mrs.* Lavenham," she said irritably, "and you know perfectly well what I'm talking about. Liam's been receiving arson threats ever since Patrick was arrested, but the police couldn't have been less interested." Her irritation got the better of her. "It's their son who's on trial, for God's sake, not them, though you'd never believe it for all the care the English police have shown them." She crunched the car into gear and drove the few yards to the churchyard entrance, where she parked in the lee of the wall and closed the window. She was preparing to open the door when it was opened from the outside.

"What are you trying to say?" demanded the policeman as she climbed out.

"What am I trying to say?" She let her accent slip into broad brogue. "Will you listen to the man? And there was me thinking my English was as good as his."

She was as tall as the constable, with striking good looks, and colour rose in her cheeks. "I didn't mean it that way, Mrs. Lavenham. I meant, are you saying it was arson?"

"Of course it was arson," she countered, securing her mane of brown hair with a band at the back of her neck and raising her coat collar against the wind which two hundred yards away was feeding the inferno. "Are you saying it wasn't?"

"Can you prove it?"

"I thought that was your job."

He opened his notebook again, looking more like an earnest student than an officer of the law. "Do you know who might have been responsible?"

She reached inside the car for her handbag. "Probably the same people who wrote 'IRISH TRASH' across their front wall," she said, slamming the door and locking it. "Or maybe it's the ones who broke into the house two weeks ago during the night and smashed Bridey's Madonna and Child before urinating all over the pieces on the carpet. Who knows?" She gave him credit for looking disturbed at what she was saying. "Look, forget it," she said wearily.

"It's late and I'm tired, and I want to get home to my children. Can you make that radio call so I don't get held up at the other end?"

"I'll do it from the car." He started to turn away, then changed his mind. "I'll be reporting what you've told me, Mrs. Lavenham, including your suggestion that the police have been negligent in their duty."

She smiled slightly. "Is that a threat or a promise, Officer?"

"It's a promise."

"Then I hope you have better luck than I've had. I might have been speaking in Gaelic for all the notice your colleagues took of my warnings." She set off for the footpath.

"You're supposed to put complaints in writing," he called after her.

"Oh, but I did," she assured him over her shoulder. "I may be Irish, but I'm not illiterate."

"I didn't mean—"

But the rest of his apology was lost on her as she rounded the corner of the church and vanished from sight.

Thursday, 18th February, 1999

It had been several days before Siobhan found the courage to confront Bridey with what the detective inspector had told her. It made her feel like a thief even to think about it. Secrets were such fragile things. Little parts of oneself that couldn't be exposed without inviting changed perceptions towards the whole. But distrust was corroding her sympathy and she needed reassurance that Bridey at least believed in Patrick's innocence.

She followed the old woman's wheelchair into the sitting room and perched on the edge of the grubby sofa that Liam always lounged upon in his oil-stained boiler suit after spending hours poking around under his unsightly wrecks. It was a mystery to Siobhan what he did under them, as none of them appeared to be driveable, and she wondered sometimes if he simply used them as a canopy under which to sleep his days away. He complained often enough that his withered right hand, which he kept tucked out of sight inside his pockets to avoid upsetting people, had deprived him of any chance of a livelihood, but the truth was, he was a lazy man who was only ever seen to rouse himself when his wife left a trailing leg as she transferred from her chair to the passenger seat of their old Ford.

"There's nothing wrong with his left hand," Cynthia Haversley would snort indignantly as she watched the regular little pantomime outside Kilkenny Cottage, "but you'd think he'd lost the use of both hands the way he carries on about his disabilities."

Privately, and with some amusement, Siobhan guessed the demonstrations were put on entirely for the benefit of the Honourable Mrs. Haversley, who made no bones about her irritation at the level of state welfare which the O'Riordans enjoyed. It was axiomatic, after all, that any woman who had enough strength in her arms to heave herself upstairs on her bottom, as Bridey did every night, could lift her own leg into a car. . . .

The Kilkenny Cottage sitting room—Bridey called it her "parlour"—was full of religious artefacts: a shrine to the Madonna and Child on the mantelpiece, a foot-high wooden cross on one wall, a print of William Holman Hunt's "The Light of the World" on another, a rosary hanging from a hook. In Siobhan, for whom religion was more of a trial than a comfort, the room invariably induced a sort of spiritual claustrophobia which made her long to get out and breathe fresh air again.

In ordinary circumstances, the paths of the O'Riordans, descendants of a roaming tinker family, and Siobhan Lavenham (nee Kerry), daughter of an Irish landowner, would never have crossed. Indeed, when she and her husband, Ian, first visited Fording Farm and fell in love with it, Siobhan had pointed out the eyesore of Kilkenny Cottage with a shudder and had predicted accurately the kind of people who were living there. Irish gypsies, she said.

"Will that make life difficult for you?" Ian had asked.

"Only if people assume we're related," she answered with a laugh, never assuming for one moment that anyone would. . . .

Bridey's habitually cowed expression reminded Siobhan of an ill-treated dog, and she put the detective inspector's accusations reluctantly, asking Bridey if she had lied about the car crash and about Patrick never striking his father. The woman wept, washing her hands in her lap as if, like Lady Macbeth, she could cleanse herself of sin.

"If I did, Siobhan, it was only to have you think well of us. You're a lovely young lady with a kind heart, but you'd not have let Patrick play with your children if you'd known what he did to his father, and you'd not have taken Rosheen into your house if you'd known her uncle Liam was a thief."

"You should have trusted me, Bridey. If I didn't ask Rosheen to leave when Patrick was arrested for murder, why would I have refused to employ her just because Liam spent time in prison?"

"Because your husband would have persuaded you against her," said Bridey truthfully. "He's never been happy about Rosheen being related to us, never mind she grew up in Ireland and hardly knew us till you said she could come here to work for you."

There was no point denying it. Ian tolerated Rosheen O'Riordan for Siobhan's sake, and because his little boys loved her, but in an ideal world he would have preferred a nanny from a more conventional background. Rosheen's relaxed attitude to child rearing, based on her own upbringing in a three-bedroomed cottage in the hills of Donegal where the children had slept four to a bed and play was adventurous, carefree, and fun, was so different from the strict supervision of his own childhood that he constantly worried about it. "They'll grow up wild," he would say. "She's not disciplining them enough." And Siobhan would look at her happy, lively, affectionate sons and wonder why the English were so fond of repression.

"He worries about his children, Bridey, more so since Patrick's arrest. We get telephone calls too, you know. Everyone knows Rosheen's his cousin."

She remembered the first such call she had taken. She had answered it in the kitchen while Rosheen was making supper for the children, and she had been shocked by the torrent of anti-Irish abuse that had poured down the line. She raised stricken eyes to Rosheen's and saw by the girl's frightened expression that it wasn't the first such call that had been made. After that, she had had an answerphone installed, and forebade Rosheen from lifting the receiver unless she was sure of the caller's identity.

Bridey's sad gaze lifted towards the Madonna on the mantelpiece. "I pray for you every day, Siobhan, just as I pray for my Patrick. God knows, I never wished this trouble on a sweet lady like you. And for why? Is it a sin to be Irish?"

Siobhan sighed to herself, hating Bridey's dreary insistence on calling her a "lady." She did not doubt Bridey's faith, nor that she prayed every day, but she doubted God's ability to undo Lavinia Fanshaw's murder eight months after the event.

And if Patrick was guilty of it, and Bridey knew he was guilty . . .

"The issue isn't about being Irish," she said bluntly, "it's about whether or not Patrick's a murderer. I'd much rather you were honest with me, Bridey. At the moment, I don't trust any of you, and that includes Rosheen. Does she know about his past? Has she been lying to me, too?" She paused, waiting for an answer, but Bridey just shook her head. "I'm not going to blame you for your son's behaviour," she said more gently, "but you can't expect me to go on pleading his cause if he's guilty."

"Indeed, and I wouldn't ask you to," said the old woman with dignity. "And you can rest your mind about Rosheen. We kept the truth to ourselves fifteen years ago. Liam wouldn't have his son blamed for something that wasn't his fault. We'll call it a car accident, he said, and may God strike me dead if I ever raise my hand in anger again." She grasped the rims of her chair wheels and slowly rotated them through half a turn. "I'll tell you honestly, though I'm a cripple and though I've been married to Liam for nearly forty years, it's only in these last fifteen that I've been able to sleep peacefully in my bed. Oh yes, Liam was a bad man, and oh yes, my Patrick lost his temper once and struck out at him, but I swear by the Mother of God that this family changed for the better the day my poor son wept for what he'd done and rang the police himself. Will you believe me, Siobhan? Will you trust an old woman when she tells you her Patrick could no more have murdered Mrs. Fanshaw than I can get out of this wheelchair and walk. To be sure, he took some jewellery from her—and to be sure, he was wrong to do it—but he was only trying to get back what had been cheated out of him."

"Except there's no proof he was cheated out of anything. The police say there's very little evidence that any odd jobs had been done in the manor. They mentioned that one or two cracks in the plaster had been filled, but not enough to indicate a contract worth three hundred pounds."

"He was up there for two weeks," said Bridey in despair. "Twelve hours a day every day."

"Then why is there nothing to show for it?"

"I don't know," said the old woman with difficulty. "All I can tell you is that he came home every night with stories about what he'd been doing. One day it was getting the heating system to work, the next re-laying the floor tiles in the kitchen where they'd come loose. It was Miss Jenkins who was telling him what needed doing, and she was thrilled to have all the little irritations sorted out once and for all."

Siobhan recalled the detective inspector's words. *"There's no one left to agree or disagree,"* he had said. *"Mrs. Fanshaw's grandson denies knowing anything about it, although he admits there might have been a private arrangement between Patrick and the nurse. She's known to have been on friendly terms with him. . . ."*

"The police are saying Patrick only invented the contract in order to explain why his fingerprints were all over the Manor House."

"That's not true."

"Are you sure? Wasn't it the first idea that came into his head when the police produced the search warrant? They questioned him for two days, Bridey, and the only explanation he gave for his fingerprints and his toolbox being in the manor was that Lavinia's nurse had asked him to sort out the dripping taps in the kitchen and bathroom. Why didn't he mention a contract earlier? Why did he wait until they found the jewellery under his floorboards before saying he was owed money?"

Teardrops watered the washing hands. "Because he's been in prison and doesn't trust the police . . . because he didn't kill Mrs. Fanshaw . . . because he was more worried about being charged with the theft of her jewellery than he was about being charged with murder. Do you think he'd have invented a contract that didn't exist? My boy isn't stupid, Siobhan. He doesn't tell stories that he can't back up. Not when he's had two whole days to think about them."

Siobhan shook her head. "Except he couldn't back it up. You're the only person, other than Patrick, who claims to know anything about it, and your word means nothing because you're his mother."

"But don't you see?" the woman pleaded. "That's why you can be sure Patrick's telling the truth. If he'd believed for one moment it would all be denied, he'd have given some other reason for why he took the jewellery. Do you hear what I'm saying? He's a good liar, Siobhan—for his sins, he always has been—and he'd not have invented a poor, weak story like the one he's been saddled with."

3.

Tuesday, 23rd June, 1998

It was a rambling defence that Patrick finally produced when it dawned on him that the police were serious about charging him with the murders. Siobhan heard both Bridey's and the inspector's versions of it, and she wasn't surprised that the police found it difficult to swallow. It depended almost entirely on the words and actions of the murdered nurse.

Patrick claimed Dorothy Jenkins had come to Kilkenny Cottage and asked him if he was willing to do some odd jobs at the Manor House for a cash sum of three hundred pounds. "I've finally persuaded her miserable skinflint of a grandson that I'll walk out one day and not come back if he doesn't do something about my working conditions, so he's agreed to pay up," she had said triumphantly. "Are you interested, Patrick? It's a bit of moonlighting . . . no VAT . . . no Inland Revenue . . . just a couple of weeks' work for money in hand. But for goodness' sake don't go talking about it," she had warned him, "or you can be sure Cynthia Haversley will notify social services that you're working and you'll lose your unemployment benefit. You know what an interfering busybody she is."

"I needed convincing she wasn't pulling a fast one," Patrick told the police. "I've been warned off in the past by that bastard grandson of Mrs. F's and the whole thing seemed bloody unlikely to me. So she takes me along to see him and he's nice as pie, shakes me by the hand and says it's a kosher contract. We'll let bygones be bygones, he says. I worked like a dog for two weeks and, yes, of course I went into Mrs. Fanshaw's bedroom. I popped in every morning because she and I were mates. I would say 'hi,' and she would giggle and say 'hi' back. And yes, I touched almost everything in the house—most of the time I was moving furniture around for Miss Jenkins. 'It's so boring when you get too old to change things,' she'd say to me. 'Let's see how that table looks in here.' Then she'd clap her hands and say: 'Isn't this exciting?' I thought she was almost as barmy as the old lady, but I wasn't going to argue with her. I mean, three hundred quid is three hundred quid, and if that's what was wanted I was happy to do the business."

On the second Saturday—"the day I was supposed to be paid . . . shit . . . I should have known it was a scam. . . ." —Mrs. Fanshaw's grandson was in the Manor House hall waiting for him when he arrived.

"I thought the bastard had come to give me my wages, but instead he accuses me of nicking a necklace. I called him a bloody liar, so he took a swing at me and landed one on my jaw. Next thing I know, I'm out the front door, facedown on the gravel. Yeah, of course that's how I got the scratches. I've never hit a woman in my life, and I certainly didn't get into a fight with either of the old biddies at the manor."

There was a two-hour hiatus during which he claimed to have driven around in a fury wondering how "to get the bastard to pay what he owed." He toyed with the idea of going to the police—"I was pretty sure Miss Jenkins would back me up, she was that mad with him, but I didn't reckon you lot could do anything, not without social services getting to hear about it, and then I'd be worse off than I was before. . . ."—but in the end he opted for more direct action and sneaked back to Sowerbridge Manor through the gate at the bottom of the garden.

"I knew Miss Jenkins would see me right if she could. And she did. 'Take this, Patrick,' she said, handing me some of Mrs. F's jewellery, 'and if there's any comeback I'll say it was my idea.' I tell you," he finished aggressively, "I'm gutted she and Mrs. F are dead. At least they treated me like a friend, which is more than can be said of the rest of Sowerbridge."

He was asked why he hadn't mentioned any of this before. "Because I'm not a fool," he said. "Word has it Mrs. F was killed for her jewellery. Do you think I'm going to admit having some of it under my floorboards when she was battered to death a few hours later?"

Thursday, 18th February, 1999

Siobhan pondered in silence for a minute or two. "Weak or not, Bridey, it's the one he has to go to trial with, and at the moment no one believes it. It would be different if he could prove any of it."

"How?"

"I don't know." She shook her head. "Did he show the jewellery to anyone *before* Lavinia was killed?"

A sly expression crept into the woman's eyes as if a new idea had suddenly occurred to her. "Only to me and Rosheen," she said, "but, as you know, Siobhan, not a word we say is believed."

"Did either of you mention it to anyone else?"

"Why would we? When all's said and done, he took the things without permission, never mind it was Miss Jenkins who gave them to him."

"Well, it's a pity Rosheen didn't tell me about it. It would make a world of difference if I could say I knew on the Saturday afternoon that Patrick already had Lavinia's necklace in his possession."

Bridey looked away towards her Madonna, crossing herself as she did so, and Siobhan knew she was lying. "She thinks the world of you, Siobhan. She'd not embarrass you by making you a party to her cousin's troubles. In any case, you'd not have been interested. Was your mind not taken up with cooking that day? Was that not the Saturday you were entertaining Mr. and Mrs. Haversley to dinner to pay off all the dinners you've had from them but never wanted?"

There were no secrets in a village, thought Siobhan, and if Bridey knew how much Ian and she detested the grinding tedium of Sowerbridge social life, which revolved around the all-too-regular "dinner party," presumably the rest of Sowerbridge did as well. "Are we really that obvious, Bridey?"

"To the Irish, maybe, but not to the English," said the old woman with a crooked smile. "The English see what they want to see. If you don't believe me, Siobhan, look at the way they've condemned my poor Patrick as a murdering thief before he's even been tried."

Siobhan had questioned Rosheen about the jewellery afterwards and, like Bridey, the girl had wrung her hands in distress. But Rosheen's distress had everything to do with her aunt's expecting her to perjure herself and nothing at all to do with the facts. "Oh, Siobhan," she had wailed, "does she expect me to stand up in court and tell lies? Because it'll not do Patrick any good when they find me out. Surely it's better to say nothing than to keep inventing stories that no one believes?"

11:55 P.M.—*Monday, 8th March, 1999*

It was cold on the footpath because the wall of The Old Vicarage was reflecting the heat back towards Kilkenny Cottage, but the sound of the burning house was deafening. The pine rafters and ceiling joists popped and exploded like intermittent rifle fire while the flames kept up a hungry roar. As Siobhan emerged onto the road leading up from the junction, she found herself in a crowd of her neighbours, who seemed to be watching the blaze in a spirit of revelry—almost, she thought in amazement, as if it were a spectacular fireworks display put on for their enjoyment.

People raised their arms and pointed whenever a new rafter caught alight, and "oohs" and "aahs" burst out of their mouths like a cheer. Any moment now, she thought cynically, and they'd bring out an effigy of that other infamous Catholic, Guy Fawkes, who was ritually burnt every year for trying to blow up the Houses of Parliament.

She started to work her way through the crowd but was stopped by Nora Bentley, the elderly doctor's wife, who caught her arm and drew her close. The Bentleys were far and away Siobhan's favourites among her neighbours, being the only ones with enough tolerance to stand against the continuous barrage of anti-O'Riordan hatred that poured from the mouths of almost everyone else. Although as Ian often pointed out, they could afford to be tolerant. "Be fair, Siobhan. Lavinia wasn't related to them. They might feel differently if she'd been *their* granny."

"We've been worried about you, my dear," said Nora. "What with all this going on, we didn't know whether you were trapped inside the farm or outside."

Siobhan gave her a quick hug. "Outside. I stayed late at work to sort out some contracts, and I've had to abandon the car at the church."

"Well, I'm afraid your drive's completely blocked with fire engines. If it's any consolation, we're all in the same boat, although Jeremy Jardine and the Haversleys have the added worry of sparks carrying on the wind and setting light to their houses." She chuckled suddenly. "You have to laugh. Cynthia bullied the firemen into taking preventative measures by hosing down the front of Malvern House, and now she's tearing strips off poor old Peter because he left their bedroom window open. The whole room's completely saturated."

Siobhan grinned. "Good," she said unsympathetically. "It's time Cynthia had some of her own medicine."

Nora wagged an admonishing finger at her. "Don't be too hard on her, my dear. For all her sins, Cynthia can be very kind when she wants to be. It's a pity you've never seen that side of her."

"I'm not sure I'd want to," said Siobhan cynically. "At a guess, she only shows it when she's offering charity. Where are they, anyway?"

"I've no idea. I expect Peter's making up the spare-room beds and Cynthia's at the front somewhere behaving like the chief constable. You know how bossy she is."

"Yes," agreed Siobhan, who had been on the receiving end of Cynthia's hectoring tongue more often than she cared to remember. Indeed, if she had any regrets about moving to Sowerbridge, they were all centred around the overbearing personality of the Honourable Mrs. Haversley.

By one of those legal quirks of which the English are so fond, the owners of Malvern House had title to the first hundred feet of Fording Farm's driveway while the owners of the farm had right of way in perpetuity across it. This had led to a state of war existing between the two households, although it was a war that had been going on long before the Lavenhams' insignificant tenure of eighteen months. Ian maintained that Cynthia's insistence on her rights stemmed from the fact that the Haversleys were, and always had been, the poor relations of the Fanshaws at the Manor House. ("You get slowly more impoverished if you inherit through the distaff side," he said, "and Peter's family had never been able to lay claim to the manor. It's made Cynthia bitter.") Nevertheless, had he and Siobhan paid heed to their solicitor's warnings, they might have questioned why such a beautiful place had had five different owners in under ten years. Instead, they had accepted the previous owners' assurances that everything in the garden was lovely—"*You'll like Cynthia Haversley. She's a charming woman.*"—and put the rapid turnover down to coincidence.

Something that sounded like a grenade detonating exploded in the heart of the fire and Nora Bentley jumped. She tapped her heart with a fluttery hand. "Goodness me, it's just like the war," she said in a rush. "*So exciting.*" She tempered this surprising statement by adding that she felt sorry for the O'Riordans, but her sympathy came a poor second to her desire for sensation.

"Are Liam and Bridey here?" asked Siobhan, looking around.

"I don't think so, dear. To be honest, I wonder if they even know what's happening. They were very secretive about where they were staying in Winchester; unless the police know where they are, well"—she shrugged—"who could have told them?"

"Rosheen knows."

Nora gave an absent-minded smile. "Yes, but she's with your boys at the farm."

"We are on the phone, Nora."

"I know, dear, but it's all been so sudden. One minute, nothing; the next, mayhem. As a matter of fact, I did suggest we call Rosheen, but Cynthia said there was no point. Let Liam and Bridey have a good night's sleep, she said. What can they do that the fire brigade haven't already done? Why bother them unnecessarily?"

"I'll bear that in mind when Cynthia's house goes up in flames," said Siobhan dryly, glancing at her watch and telling herself to get a move on. Curiosity held her back. "When did it start?"

"No one knows," said Nora. "Sam and I smelt burning about an hour and a half ago and came to investigate, but by that time the flames were already at the downstairs windows." She waved an arm at The Old Vicarage. "We knocked up Jeremy and got him to call the fire brigade, but the whole thing was out of control long before they arrived."

Siobhan's eyes followed the waving arm. "Why didn't Jeremy call them earlier? Surely he'd have smelt burning before you did? He lives right opposite." Her glance travelled on to the Bentleys' house, Rose Cottage, which stood behind The Old Vicarage, a good hundred yards distant from Kilkenny Cottage.

Nora looked anxious, as if she, too, found Jeremy Jardine's inertia suspicious. "He says he didn't, says he was in his cellar. He was horrified when he saw what was going on."

Siobhan took that last sentence with a pinch of salt. Jeremy Jardine was a wine shipper who had used his Fanshaw family connection some years before to buy The Old Vicarage off the church commissioners for its extensive cellars. But the beautiful brick house looked out over the O'Riordans' unsightly wrecking ground, and he was one of their most strident critics. No one knew how much he'd paid for it, although rumour suggested it had been sold off at a fifth of its value. Certainly questions had been asked at the time about why a substantial Victorian rectory had never been advertised for sale on the open market, although, as usual in Sowerbridge, answers were difficult to come by when they involved the Fanshaw family.

Prior to the murders, Siobhan had been irritated enough by Jeremy's unremitting criticism of the O'Riordans to ask him why he'd bought The Old Vicarage, knowing what the view was going to be. "It's not as though you didn't know about Liam's cars," she told him. "Nora Bentley says you'd been living with Lavinia at the manor for two years before the purchase." He'd muttered darkly about good investments turning sour when promises of action failed to materialise and she had interpreted this as meaning he'd paid a pittance to acquire the property from the church on the mistaken understanding that one of his district councillor buddies could force the O'Riordans to clean up their frontage.

Ian had laughed when she told him about the conversation. "Why on earth doesn't he just offer to pay for the cleanup himself? Liam's never going to pay to have those blasted wrecks removed, but he'd be pleased as punch if someone else did."

"Perhaps he can't afford it. Nora says the Fanshaws aren't half as well off as everyone believes, and Jeremy's business is no great shakes. I know he talks grandly about how he supplies all the top families with quality wine, but that case he sold us was rubbish."

"It wouldn't cost much, not if a scrap-metal merchant did it."

Siobhan had wagged a finger at him. "You know what your problem is, husband of mine? You're too sensible to live in Sowerbridge. Also, you're ignoring the fact that there's an issue of principle at stake. If Jeremy pays for the cleanup then the O'Riordans will have won. Worse still, they will be seen to have won because *their* house will also rise in value the minute the wrecks go."

He shook his head. "Just promise me you won't start taking sides, Shiv. You're no keener on the O'Riordans than anyone else, and there's no law that says the Irish have to stick together. Life's too short to get involved in their ridiculous feuds."

"I promise," she had said, and at the time she had meant it.

But that was before Patrick had been charged with murder. . . .

There was no doubt in the minds of most of Sowerbridge's inhabitants that Patrick O'Riordan saw Lavinia Fanshaw as an easy target. In November, two years previously, he had relieved the confused old woman of a Chippendale chair worth five hundred pounds after claiming a European directive required all hedgerows to be clipped to a uniform standard. He had stripped her laurels to within four feet of the ground in return for the antique, and had sold the foliage on to a crony who made festive Christmas wreaths.

Nor had he shown any remorse. "It was a bit of business," he said in the pub afterwards, grinning happily as he swilled his beer, "and she was pleased as punch about it. She told me she's always hated that chair." He was a small, wiry man with a shock of dark hair and penetrating blue eyes which stared unwaveringly at the person he was talking to—like a fighting dog whose intention was to intimidate. "In any case, I did this village a favour. The manor looks a damn sight better since I sorted the frontage."

The fact that most people agreed with him was neither here nor there. The combination of Lavinia's senility and extraordinary longevity meant Sowerbridge Manor was rapidly falling into disrepair, but this did not entitle anyone, least of all an O'Riordan, to take advantage of her. What about Kilkenny Cottage's frontage? people protested. Liam's cars were a great deal worse than Lavinia's overgrown hedge. There was even suspicion that her live-in nurse had connived in the fraud, because she was known to be extremely critical of the deteriorating conditions in which she was expected to work.

"I can't be watching Mrs. Fanshaw twenty-four hours a day," Dorothy Jenkins had said firmly, "and if she makes an arrangement behind my back, then there's nothing I can do about it. It's her grandson you should be talking to. He's the one with power of attorney over her affairs, but he's never going to sell this place before she's dead because he's too mean to put her in a nursing home. She could live forever the way she's going, and nursing homes cost far more than I do. He pays me peanuts because he says I'm getting free board and lodging, but there's no heating, the roof leaks, and the whole place is a death trap of rotten floorboards. He's only waiting for the poor old thing to die so that he can sell the land to a property developer and live in clover for the rest of his life."

Monday, 8th March, 1999

The crowd seemed to be growing bigger and more boisterous by the minute, but as Siobhan recognised few of the faces, she realised word of the fire must have spread to surrounding villages. She couldn't understand why the police were letting thrill-seekers through until she heard one man say that he'd parked on the Southampton Road and cut across a field to bypass the police block. There was much jostling for position; the smell of beer on the breath of one man who pushed past her was overpowering. He barged against her and she jabbed him angrily in the ribs with a sharp elbow before taking Nora's arm and shepherding her across the road.

"Someone's going to be hurt in a minute," she said. "They've obviously come straight from the pub." She manoeuvred through a knot of people beside the wall of Malvern House, and ahead of her she saw Nora's husband, Dr. Sam Bentley, talking with Peter and Cynthia Haversley. "There's Sam. I'll leave you with him and then be on my way. I'm worried about Rosheen and the boys." She nodded briefly to the Haversleys, raised a hand in greeting to Sam Bentley, then prepared to push on.

"You won't get through," said Cynthia forcefully, planting her corseted body between Siobhan and the crossroads. "They've barricaded the entire junction and no one's allowed past." Her face had turned crimson from the heat, and Siobhan wondered if she had any idea how unattractive she looked. The combination of dyed blond hair atop a glistening beetroot complexion was reminiscent of sherry trifle, and Siobhan wished she had a camera to record the fact. Siobhan knew her to be in her late sixties because Nora had let slip once that she and Cynthia shared a birthday, but Cynthia herself preferred to draw a discreet veil over her age. Privately (and rather grudgingly) Siobhan admitted she had a case, because her plumpness gave her skin a smooth, firm quality which made her look considerably younger than her years, though it didn't make her any more likeable.

Siobhan had asked Ian once if he thought her antipathy to Cynthia was an "Irish thing." The idea had amused him. "On what basis? Because the Honourable Mrs. Haversley symbolises colonial authority?"

"Something like that."

"Don't be absurd, Shiv. She's a fat snob with a power complex who loves throwing her weight around. No one likes her. I certainly don't. She probably wouldn't be so bad if her wet husband had ever stood up to her, but poor old Peter's as cowed as everyone else. You should learn to ignore her. In the great scheme of things, she's about as relevant as birdshit on your windscreen."

"I *hate* birdshit on my windscreen."

"I know," he had said with a grin, "but you don't assume pigeons single your car out because you're Irish, do you?"

She made an effort now to summon a pleasant smile as she answered Cynthia. "Oh, I'm sure they'll make an exception of me. Ian's in Italy this week, which means Rosheen and the boys are on their own. I think I'll be allowed through in the circumstances."

"If you aren't," said Dr. Bentley, "Peter and I can give you a leg-up over the wall and you can cut through Malvern House garden."

"Thank you." She studied his face for a moment. "Does anyone know how the fire started, Sam?"

"We think Liam must have left a cigarette burning."

Siobhan pulled a wry face. "Then it must have been the slowest-burning cigarette in history," she said. "They were gone by nine o'clock this morning."

He looked as worried as his wife had done earlier. "It's only a guess."

"Oh, come on! If it was a smouldering cigarette you'd have seen flames at the windows by lunchtime." She turned her attention back to Cynthia. "I'm surprised that Sam and Nora smelt burning before you did," she said with deliberate lightness. "You and Peter are so much closer than they are."

"We probably would have done if we'd been here," said Cynthia, "but we went to supper with friends in Salisbury. We didn't get home until after Jeremy called the fire brigade." She stared Siobhan down, daring her to dispute the statement.

"Matter of fact," said Peter, "we only just scraped in before the police arrived with barricades. Otherwise they'd have made us leave the car at the church."

Siobhan wondered if the friends had invited the Haversleys or if the Haversleys had invited themselves. She guessed the latter. None of the O'Riordans' neighbours would have wanted to save Kilkenny Cottage, and unlike Jeremy, she thought sarcastically, the Haversleys had no cellar to skulk in. "I really must go," she said then. "Poor Rosheen will be worried sick." But if she expected sympathy for Liam and Bridey's niece, she didn't get it.

"If she were *that* worried, she'd have come down here," declared Cynthia. "With or without your boys. I don't know why you employ her. She's one of the laziest and most deceitful creatures I've ever met. Frankly, I wouldn't have her for love or money."

Siobhan smiled slightly. It was like listening to a cracked record, she thought. The day the Honourable

Mrs. Haversley resisted an opportunity to snipe at an O'Riordan would be a red-letter day in Siobhan's book. "I suspect the feeling's mutual, Cynthia. Threat of death might persuade her to work for you, but not love or money."

Cynthia's retort, a pithy one if her annoyed expression was anything to go by, was swallowed by the sound of Kilkenny Cottage collapsing inwards upon itself as the beams supporting the roof finally gave way. There was a shout of approval from the crowd behind them, and while everyone else's attention was temporarily distracted, Siobhan watched Peter Haversley give his wife a surreptitious pat on the back.

4.

Saturday, 30th January, 1999

Siobhan had stubbornly kept an open mind about Patrick's guilt, although as she was honest enough to admit to Ian, it was more for Rosheen and Bridey's sake than because she seriously believed there was room for reasonable doubt. She couldn't forget the fear she had seen in Rosheen's eyes one day when she came home early to find Jeremy Jardine at the front door of the farm. "What are you doing here?"

she had demanded of him angrily, appalled by the ashen colour in her nanny's cheeks.

There was a telling silence before Rosheen stumbled into words.

"He says we're murdering Mrs. Fanshaw all over again by taking Patrick's side," said the girl in a shaken voice. "I said it was wrong to condemn him before the evidence is heard—you told me everyone would believe Patrick was innocent until the trial—but Mr. Jardine just keeps shouting at me."

Jeremy had laughed. "I'm doing the rounds with my new wine list," he said, jerking his thumb towards his car. "But I'm damned if I'll stay quiet while an Irish murderer's cousin quotes English law at me."

Siobhan had controlled her temper because her two sons were watching from the kitchen window. "Go inside now," she told Rosheen, "but if Mr. Jardine comes here again when Ian and I are at work, I want you to phone the police immediately." She waited while the girl retreated with relief into the depths of the house. "I mean it, Jeremy," she said coldly. "However strongly you may feel about all of this, I'll have you prosecuted if you try that trick again. It's not as though Rosheen has any evidence that can help Patrick, so you're simply wasting your time."

He shrugged. "You're a fool, Siobhan. Patrick's guilty as sin. You know it. Everyone knows it. Just don't come crying to me later when the jury proves us right and you find yourself tarred with the same brush as the O'Riordans."

"I already have been," she said curtly. "If you and the Haversleys had your way, I'd have been lynched by now, but, God knows, I'd give my right arm to see Patrick get off, if only to watch the three of you wearing sackcloth and ashes for the rest of your lives."

Ian had listened to her account of the conversation with a worried frown on his face. "It won't help Patrick if he does get off," he warned. "No one's going to believe he didn't do it. Reasonable doubt sounds all very well in court, but it won't count for anything in Sowerbridge. He'll never be able to come back."

"I know."

"Then don't get too openly involved," he advised. "We'll be living here for the foreseeable future, and I really don't want the boys growing up in an atmosphere of hostility. Support Bridey and Rosheen by all means"—he gave her a wry smile—"but do me a favour, Shiv, and hold that Irish temper of yours in check. I'm not convinced Patrick is worth going to war over, particularly not with our close neighbours."

It was good advice, but difficult to follow. There was too much overt prejudice against the Irish in general for

Siobhan to stay quiet indefinitely. War finally broke out at one of Cynthia and Peter Haversley's tedious dinner parties at Malvern House, which were impossible to avoid without telling so many lies that it was easier to attend the wretched things. "She watches the driveway from her window," sighed Siobhan when Ian asked why they couldn't just say they had another engagement that night. "She keeps tabs on everything we do. She knows when we're in and when we're out. It's like living in a prison."

"I don't know why she keeps inviting us," he said.

Siobhan found his genuine ignorance of Cynthia's motives amusing. "It's her favourite sport," she said matter-of-factly. "Bearbaiting . . . with me as the bear."

Ian sighed. "Then let's tell her the truth, say we'd rather stay in and watch television."

"Good idea. There's the phone. *You* tell her."

He smiled unhappily. "It'll make her even more impossible."

"Of course it will."

"Perhaps we should just grit our teeth and go."

"Why not? It's what we usually do."

The evening had been a particularly dire one, with Cynthia and Jeremy holding the platform as usual, Peter getting quietly drunk, and the Bentleys making only occasional remarks. A silence had developed round the table and Siobhan, who had been firmly biting her tongue since they arrived, consulted her watch under cover of her napkin and wondered if nine forty-five was too early to announce departure.

"I suppose what troubles me the most," said Jeremy suddenly, "is that if I'd pushed to have the O'Riordans evicted years ago, poor old Lavinia would still be alive." He was a similar age to the Lavenhams and handsome in a florid sort of way—*Too much sampling of his own wares,* Siobhan always thought—and loved to style himself as Hampshire's most eligible bachelor. Many was the time Siobhan had wanted to ask why, if he was so eligible, he remained unattached, but she didn't bother because she thought she knew the answer. He couldn't find a woman stupid enough to agree with his own valuation of himself.

"You can't evict people from their own homes," Sam Bentley pointed out mildly. "On that basis, we could all be evicted any time our neighbours took against us."

"Oh, you know what I mean," Jeremy answered, looking pointedly at Siobhan as if to remind her that she was tarred with the O'Riordans' brush. "There must be something I could have done—had them prosecuted for environmental pollution, perhaps?"

"We should never have allowed them to come here in the first place," declared Cynthia. "It's iniquitous that the rest of us have no say over what sort of people will be living on our doorsteps. If the Parish Council was allowed to vet prospective newcomers, the problem would never have arisen."

Siobhan raised her head and smiled in amused disbelief at the other woman's arrogant assumption that the Parish Council was in her pocket. "What a good idea!" she said brightly, ignoring Ian's warning look across the table. "It would also give prospective newcomers a chance to vet the people already living here. It means house prices would drop like a stone, of course, but at least neither side could say afterwards that they went into it with their eyes closed."

The pity was that Cynthia was too stupid to understand irony. "You're quite wrong, my dear," she said with a condescending smile. "The house prices would go *up*. They always do when an area becomes exclusive."

"Only when there are enough purchasers who want the kind of exclusivity you're offering them, Cynthia. It's basic economics." Siobhan proped her elbows on the table and leaned forward, stung into pricking the fat woman's self-righteous bubble once and for all, even if she did recognise that her real target was Jeremy Jardine. "And for what it's worth, there won't be any competition to live in Sowerbridge when word gets out that, *however* much money you have, there's no point in applying unless you share the Fanshaw mafia's belief that Hitler was right."

Nora Bentley gave a small gasp and made damping gestures with her hands.

Jeremy was less restrained. "Well, my God!" he burst out aggressively. "That's bloody rich coming from an Irishwoman. Where was Ireland in the war? Sitting on the sidelines, rooting for Germany, that's where. And you have the damn nerve to sit in judgment on us! All you Irish are despicable. You flood over here like a plague of sewer rats looking for handouts, then you criticise us when we point out that we don't think you're worth the trouble you're causing us."

It was like a simmering saucepan boiling over. In the end, all that had been achieved by restraint was to allow resentment to fester. On both sides.

"I suggest you withdraw those remarks, Jeremy," said Ian coldly, rousing himself in defence of his wife. "You might be entitled to insult Siobhan like that if your business paid as much tax and employed as many people as hers does, but as that's never going to happen I think you should apologise."

"No way. Not unless she apologises to Cynthia first."

Once roused, Ian's temper was even more volatile than his wife's. "She's got nothing to apologise for," he snapped. "Everything she said was true. Neither you nor Cynthia has any more right than anyone else to dictate what goes on in this village, yet you do it anyway. And with very little justification. At least the rest of us bought our houses fair and square on the open market, which is more than can be said of you or Peter. He inherited his, and you got yours cheap via the old-boy network. I just hope you're prepared for the consequences when something goes wrong. You can't incite hatred and then pretend you're not responsible for it."

"Now, now, now!" said Sam with fussy concern. "This sort of talk isn't healthy."

"Sam's right," said Nora. "What's said can never be unsaid."

Ian shrugged. "Then tell this village to keep its collective mouth shut about the Irish in general and the O'Riordans in particular. Or doesn't the rule apply to them? Perhaps it's only the well-to-do English like the Haversleys and Jeremy who can't be criticised?"

Peter Haversley gave an unexpected snigger. "Well-to-do?" he muttered tipsily. "Who's well-to-do? We're all in hock up to our blasted eyeballs while we wait for the manor to be sold."

"Be quiet, Peter," said his wife.

But he refused to be silenced. "That's the trouble with murder. Everything gets so damned messy. You're not allowed to sell what's rightfully yours because probate goes into limbo." His bleary eyes looked across the table at Jeremy. "It's your fault, you sanctimonious little toad. Power of bloody attorney, my arse. You're too damn greedy for your own good. Always were . . . always will be. I kept telling you to put the old bloodsucker into a home but would you listen? Don't worry, you kept saying, she'll be dead soon. . . ."

00:23 A.M.—*Tuesday, 9th March, 1999*

The hall lights were on in the farmhouse when Siobhan finally reached it, but there was no sign of Rosheen. This surprised her until she checked the time and saw that it was well after midnight. She went into the kitchen and squatted down to stroke Patch, the O'Riordans' amiable mongrel, who lifted his head from the hearth in front of the Aga and wagged his stumpy tail before giving an enormous yawn and returning to his slumbers. Siobhan had agreed to look after him while the O'Riordans were away and he seemed entirely at home in his new surroundings. She peered out of the kitchen window towards the fire, but there was nothing to see except the dark line of trees bordering the property, and it occurred to her then that Rosheen probably had no idea her uncle's house had gone up in flames.

She tiptoed upstairs to check on her two young sons, who, woke briefly to wrap their arms around her neck and acknowledge her kisses before closing their eyes again. She paused outside Rosheen's room for a moment, hoping to hear the sound of the girl's television, but there was only silence and she retreated downstairs again, relieved to be spared explanations tonight. Rosheen had been frightened enough by the anti-Irish slogans daubed across the front of Kilkenny Cottage; God only knew how she would react to hearing it had been destroyed.

Rosheen's employment with them had happened more by accident than design when Siobhan's previous nanny—a young woman given to melodrama—had announced after two weeks in rural Hampshire that she'd rather "die" than spend another night away from the lights of London. In desperation, Siobhan had taken up Bridey's shy suggestion to fly Rosheen over from Ireland on a month's trial—"*She's Liam's brother's daughter and she's a wonder with children. She's been looking after her brothers and her cousins since she was knee-high to a grasshopper, and they all think the world of her.*"—and Siobhan had been surprised by how quickly and naturally the girl had fitted into the household.

Ian had reservations—"*She's too young . . . she's too scatter-brained . . . I'm not sure I want to be quite so cosy with the O'Riordans.*"—but he had come to respect her in the wake of Patrick's arrest when, despite the hostility in the village, she had refused to abandon either Siobhan or Bridey. "Mind you, I wouldn't bet on family loyalty being what's keeping her here," he added nonetheless.

"What else is there?"

"Sex with Kevin Wyllie. She goes weak at the knees every time she sees him, never mind he's probably intimately acquainted with the thugs who're terrorising Liam and Bridey."

"You can't blame him for that. He's lived here all his life. I should imagine most of Sowerbridge could name names if they wanted to. At least he's had the guts to stand by Rosheen."

"He's an illiterate oaf with an IQ of ten," growled Ian. "Rosheen's not stupid, so what the hell do they find to talk about?"

Siobhan giggled. "I don't think his conversation is what interests her."

Recognising that she was too hyped-up to sleep, she poured herself a glass of wine and played the messages on the answerphone. There were a couple of business calls followed by one from Ian. "*Hi, it's me. Things are progressing well on the Ravenelli front. All being well, hand-printed Italian silk should be on offer through Lavenham Interiors by August. Good news, eh? I can think of at least two projects that will benefit from the designs they've been showing me. You'll love them, Shiv. Aquamarine swirls with every shade of terra cotta you can imagine.*" Pause for a yawn. "*I'm missing you and the boys like crazy. Give me a ring if you get back before eleven, otherwise I'll speak to you tomorrow. I should be home on Friday.*" He finished with a slobbery kiss which made her laugh.

The last message was from Liam O'Riordan and had obviously been intercepted by Rosheen. "*Hello? Are you there, Rosheen? It's . . .*" said Liam's voice before it was cut off by the receiver's being lifted. Out of curiosity, Siobhan pressed one-four-seven-one to find out when Liam had phoned, and she listened in perplexity as the computerised voice at the other end gave the time of the last call as "twenty thirty-six hours," and the number from which it was made as "eight-two-seven-five-three-eight." She knew the sequence off by heart but flicked through the telephone index anyway to make certain. *Liam & Bridey O'Riordan, Kilkenny Cottage, Sowerbridge, Tel: 827538.*

For the second time that night her fist instinct was to rush towards denial. It was a mistake, she told herself. . . . Liam couldn't possibly have been phoning from Kilkenny Cottage at eight-thirty. . . . The O'Riordans were under police protection in Winchester for the duration of Patrick's trial. . . . Kilkenny Cottage was empty when the fire started. . . .

But, oh dear God! Supposing it wasn't?

"Rosheen!" she shouted, running up the stairs again and hammering on the nanny's door. "Rosheen! It's Siobhan. Wake up! Was Liam in the cottage?" She thrust open the door and switched on the light, only to look around the room in dismay because no one was there.

Wednesday, 10th February, 1999

Siobhan had raised the question of Lavinia Fanshaw's heirs with the detective inspector. "You can't ignore the fact that both Peter Haversley and Jeremy Jardine had a far stronger motive than Patrick could ever have had," she pointed out. "They both stood to inherit from her will, and neither of them made any bones about wanting her dead. Lavinia's husband had one sister, now dead, who produced a single child, Peter, who has no children. And Lavinia's only child, a daughter, also dead, produced Jeremy, who's never married."

He was amused by the extent of her research. "We didn't ignore it, Mrs. Lavenham. It was the first thing we looked at, but you know better than anyone that they couldn't have done it because you and your husband supplied their alibis."

"Only from eight o'clock on Saturday night until two o'clock on Sunday morning," protested Siobhan. "And not out of choice either. Have you an idea what it's like living in a village like Sowerbridge, Inspector? Dinner parties are considered intrinsically superior to staying in of a Friday or Saturday night and watching telly, never mind the same boring people get invited every time and the same boring conversations take place. It's a status thing." She gave a sarcastic shrug. "Personally, I'd rather watch a good Arnie or Sly movie any day than have to appear interested in someone else's mortgage or pension plan, but then—*hell*—I'm Irish and everyone knows the Irish are common as muck."

"You'll have status enough when Patrick comes to trial," said the inspector with amusement. "You'll be the one providing the alibis."

"I wouldn't be able to if we'd managed to get rid of Jeremy and the Haversleys any sooner. Believe me, it wasn't Ian and I who kept them there—we did everything we could to make them go—they just refused to take the hints. Sam and Nora Bentley went at a reasonable time, but we couldn't get the rest of them to budge. Are you *sure* Lavinia was killed between eleven and midnight? Don't you find it suspicious that it's *my* evidence that's excluded Peter and Jeremy from the case? Everyone knows I'm the only person in Sowerbridge who'd rather give Patrick O'Riordan an alibi if I possibly could."

"What difference does that make?"

"It means I'm a reluctant witness, and therefore gives my evidence in Peter and Jeremy's favour more weight."

The inspector shook his head. "I think you're making too much of your position in all of this, Mrs. Lavenham. If Mr. Haversley and Mr. Jardine had conspired to murder Mrs. Fanshaw, wouldn't they have taken themselves to—say, Ireland—for the weekend? That would have given them a much stronger alibi than spending six hours in the home of a hostile witness. In any case," he went on apologetically, "we are sure about the time of the murders. These days, pathologists' timings are extremely precise, particularly when the bodies are found as quickly as these ones were."

Siobhan wasn't ready to give up so easily. "But you must see how odd it is that it happened the night Ian and I gave a dinner party. We *hate* dinner parties. Most of our entertaining is done around barbecues in the summer when friends come to stay. It's always casual and always spur-of-the-moment and I can't believe it was coincidence that Lavinia was murdered on the one night in the whole damn year for which we'd sent out invitations"—her mouth twisted—"*six weeks in advance. . . .*"

He eyed her thoughtfully. "If you can tell me how they did it, I might agree with you."

"Before they came to our house or after they left it," she suggested. "The pathologist's timings are wrong."

He pulled a piece of paper from a pile on his desk and turned it towards her. "That's an itemised British Telecom list of every call made from Sowerbridge Manor during the week leading up to the murders." He touched the last number. "This one was made by Dorothy Jenkins

to a friend of hers in London and was timed at ten-thirty
P.M. on the night she died. The duration time was just
over three minutes. We've spoken to the friend and she
described Miss Jenkins as at 'the end of her tether.' Apparently Mrs. Fanshaw was a difficult patient to nurse—
Alzheimer's sufferers usually are—and Miss Jenkins had
phoned this woman—also a nurse—to tell her that she
felt like 'smothering the old bitch where she lay.' It had
happened several times before, but this time Miss Jenkins
was in tears and rang off abruptly when her friend said
she had someone with her and couldn't talk for long." He
paused for a moment. "The friend was worried enough
to phone back after her visitor had gone," he went on,
"and she estimates the time of that call at about a quarter
past midnight. The line was engaged so she couldn't get
through, and she admits to being relieved because she
thought it meant Miss Jenkins had found someone else
to confide in."

Siobhan frowned. "Well, at least it proves she was
alive after midnight, doesn't it?"

The inspector shook his head. "I'm afraid not. The
phone in the kitchen had been knocked off its rest—we
think Miss Jenkins may have been trying to dial nine-nine-
nine when she was attacked"—he tapped his finger on the
piece of paper—"which means that, with or without the
pathologist's timings, she must have been killed between

that last itemised call at ten-thirty and her friend's return call at fifteen minutes past midnight, when the phone was already off the hook."

5.

00:32 A.M.—Tuesday, 9th March, 1999

Even as Siobhan lifted the receiver to call the police and report Rosheen missing, she was having second thoughts. They hadn't taken a blind bit of notice in the past, she thought bitterly, so why should it be different today? She could even predict how the conversation would go simply because she had been there so many times before.

Calm down, Mrs. Lavenham. . . . It was undoubtedly a hoax. . . . Let's see now . . . didn't someone phone you not so long ago pretending to be Bridey in the throes of a heart attack . . . ? We rushed an ambulance to her only to find her alive and well and watching television. . . . You and your nanny are Irish. . . . Someone thought it would be entertaining to get a rise out of you by creeping into Kilkenny Cottage and making a call. . . . Everyone knows the O'Riordans are notoriously careless about locking their back door. . . . Sadly we can't legislate for practical jokes. . . . Your nanny . . . ? She'll be watching the fire along with everyone else. . . .

With a sigh of frustration, she replaced the receiver and listened to the message again. "*Hello? Are you there, Rosheen? It's . . .*"

She had been so sure it was Liam the first time she heard it, but now she was less certain. The Irish accent was the easiest accent in the world to ape, and Liam's was so broad any fool could do it. For want of someone more sensible to talk to, she telephoned Ian in his hotel bedroom in Rome. "It's me," she said, "and I've only just got back. I'm sorry to wake you but they've burnt Kilkenny Cottage and Rosheen's missing. Do you think I should phone the police?"

"Hang on," he said sleepily. "Run that one by me again. Who's they?"

"I don't know," she said in frustration. "Someone—anyone—Peter Haversley patted Cynthia on the back when the roof caved in. If I knew where the O'Riordans were I'd phone them, but Rosheen's the only one who knows the number—and she's not here. I'd go back to the fire if I had a car—the village is swarming with policemen—but I've had to leave mine at the church and yours is at Heathrow—and the children will never be able to walk all the way down the drive, not at this time of night."

He gave a long yawn. "You're going much too fast. I've only just woken up. What's this about Kilkenny Cottage burning down?"

She explained it slowly.

"So where's Rosheen?" He sounded more alert now. "And what the hell was she doing leaving the boys?"

"I don't know." She told him about the telephone call from Kilkenny Cottage. "If it was Liam, Rosheen may have gone up there to see him, and now I'm worried they were in the house when the fire started. Everyone thinks it was empty because we watched them go this morning." She described the scene for him as Liam helped Bridey into their Ford Estate then drove unsmilingly past the group of similarly unsmiling neighbours who had gathered at the crossroads to see them off. "It was awful," she said. "I went down to collect Patch, and bloody Cynthia started hissing at them so the rest joined in. I really hate them, Ian."

He didn't answer immediately. "Look," he said then, "the fire brigade don't just take people's words for this kind of thing. They'll have checked to make sure there was no one in the house as soon as they got there. And if Liam and Bridey *did* come back, their car would have been parked at the front and someone would have noticed it. Okay, I agree the village is full of bigots, but they're not murderers, Shiv, and they wouldn't keep quiet if they thought the O'Riordans were burning to death. Come on, think about it. You know I'm right."

"What about Rosheen?"

"Yes, well," he said dryly, "it wouldn't be the first time, would it? Did you check the barn? I expect she's out there getting laid by Kevin Wyllie."

"She's only done it once."

"She's used the barn once," he corrected her, "but it's anyone's guess how often she's been laid by Kevin. I'll bet you a pound to a penny they're tucked up together somewhere and she'll come wandering in with a smile on her face when you least expect it. I hope you tear strips off her for it, too. She's no damn business to leave the boys on their own."

She let it ride, unwilling to be drawn into another argument about Rosheen's morals. Ian worked on the principle that what the eye didn't see the heart didn't grieve over, and refused to recognise the hypocrisy of his position, while Siobhan's view was that Kevin was merely the bit of "rough" that was keeping Rosheen amused while she looked for something better. *God knew every woman did it. . . . The road to respectability was far from straight. . . .* In any case, she agreed with his final sentiment. Even if it was Liam who phoned from the cottage, Rosheen's first responsibility was to James and Oliver. "So what should I do? Just wait for her to come back?"

"I don't see you have much choice. She's over twenty-one so the police won't do anything tonight."

"Okay."

He knew her too well. "You don't sound convinced."

She wasn't, but then she was more relaxed about the way Rosheen conducted herself than he was. The fact that they'd come home early one night and caught her in the barn with her knickers down had offended Ian deeply, even though Rosheen had been monitoring the boys all the time via a two-way transmitter that she'd taken with her. Ian had wanted to sack her on the spot, but Siobhan had persuaded him out of it after extracting a promise from Rosheen that the affair would be confined to her spare time in the future. Afterwards, and because she was a great deal less puritanical than her English husband, Siobhan had buried her face in her pillow to stifle her laughter. Her view was that Rosheen had shown typical Irish tact by having sex outside in the barn rather than under the Lavenhams' roof. As she pointed out to Ian: "*We'd never have known Kevin was there if she'd smuggled him into her room and told him to perform quietly.*"

"It's just that I'm tired," she lied, knowing she could never describe her sense of foreboding down the telephone to someone over a thousand miles away. Empty houses gave her the shivers at the best of times—a throwback to the rambling, echoing mansion of her childhood, which her overactive imagination had peopled with giants and spectres. . . . "Look, go back to sleep and I'll ring you tomorrow. It'll have sorted itself out by then. Just make sure you come home on Friday," she ended severely, "or I'll file for divorce immediately. I didn't marry you to be deserted for the Ravenelli brothers."

"I will," he promised.

Siobhan listened to the click as he hung up at the other end, then replaced her own receiver before opening the front door and looking towards the dark shape of the barn. She searched for a chink of light between the double doors but knew she was wasting her time even while she was doing it. Rosheen had been so terrified by Ian's threat to tell her parents in Ireland what she'd been up to that her sessions with Kevin were now confined to somewhere a great deal more private than Fording Farm's barn.

With a sigh she retreated to the kitchen and settled on a cushion in front of the Aga with Patch's head lying scross her lap and the bottle of wine beside her. It was another ten minutes before she noticed that the key to Kilkenny Cottage, which should have been hanging from a hook on the dresser, was no longer there.

Wednesday, 10th February, 1999

"But why are you so sure it was Patrick?" Siobhan had asked the inspector then. "Why not a total stranger? I mean, anyone could have taken the hammer from his toolbox if he'd left it in the kitchen the way he says he did."

"Because there were no signs of a break-in. Whoever killed them either had a key to the front door or was let in by Dorothy Jenkins. And that means it must have been someone she knew."

"Maybe she hadn't locked up," said Siobhan, clutching at straws. "Maybe they came in through the back door."

"Have you ever tried to open the back door to the manor, Mrs. Lavenham?"

"No."

"Apart from the fact that the bolts were rusted into their sockets, it's so warped and swollen with damp you have to put a shoulder to it to force it ajar, and it screams like a banshee every time you do it. If a stranger had come in through the back door at eleven o'clock at night, he wouldn't have caught Miss Jenkins in the kitchen. She'd have taken to her heels the minute she heard the banshee-wailing and would have used one of the phones upstairs to call the police."

"You can't know that," argued Siobhan. "Sowerbridge is the sleepiest place on earth. Why would she assume it was an intruder? She probably thought it was Jeremy paying a late-night visit to his grandmother."

"We don't think so." He picked up a pen and turned it between his fingers. "As far as we can establish, that door was never used. Certainly none of the neighbours report going in that way. The milkman said Miss Jenkins kept it bolted because on the one occasion when she tried to open it, it became so wedged that she had to ask him to force it shut again."

She sighed, admitting defeat. "Patrick's always been so sweet to me and my children. I just can't believe he's a murderer."

He smiled at her naivete. "The two are not mutually exclusive, Mrs. Lavenham. I expect Jack the Ripper's neighbour said the same about him."

01:00 A.M.—*Tuesday, 9th March, 1999*

People began to shiver as the smouldering remains were dowsed by the fire hoses and the pungent smell of wet ashes stung their nostrils. In the aftermath of excitement, a sense of shame crept among the inhabitants of Sowerbridge— *schadenfreude* was surely alien to their natures?—and bit by bit the crowd began to disperse. Only the Haversleys, the Bentleys, and Jeremy Jardine lingered at the crossroads, held by a mutual fascination for the scene of devastation that would greet them every time they emerged from their houses.

"We won't be able to open our windows for weeks," said Nora Bentley, wrinkling her nose. "The smell will be suffocating."

"It'll be worse when the wind gets up and deposits soot all over the place," complained Peter Haversley, brushing ash from his coat.

His wife clicked her tongue impatiently. "We'll just have to put up with it," she said. "It's hardly the end of the world."

Sam Bentley surprised her with a sudden bark of laughter. "Well spoken, Cynthia, considering you'll be bearing the brunt of it. The prevailing winds are southwesterly, which means most of the muck will collect in Malvern House. Still"—he paused to glance from her to Peter—"you sow a wind and you reap a whirlwind, eh?"

There was a short silence.

"Have you noticed how Liam's wrecks have survived intact?" asked Nora then, with assumed brightness. "Is it a judgment, do you think?"

"Don't be ridiculous," said Jeremy.

Sam gave another brief chortle. "Is it ridiculous? You complained enough when there were only the cars to worry about. Now you've got a burnt-out cottage to worry about as well. I can't believe the O'Riordans were insured, so it'll be years before anything is done. If you're lucky, a developer will buy the land and build an estate of little boxes on your doorstep. If you're unlucky, Liam will put up a corrugated- iron shack and live in that. And do you know, Jeremy, I hope he does. Personal revenge is so much sweeter than anything the law can offer."

"What's that supposed to mean?"

"You'd have been wiser to call the fire brigade earlier," said the old doctor bluntly. "Nero may have fiddled while Rome burned, but it didn't do his reputation any good."

Another silence.

"What are you implying?" demanded Cynthia aggressively. "That Jeremy could somehow have prevented the fire?"

Jeremy Jardine folded his arms. "I'll sue you for slander if you *are*, Sam."

"It won't be just me. Half the village is wondering why Nora and I smelt burning before you did, and why Cynthia and Peter took themselves off to Salisbury on a Monday evening for the first time in living memory."

"Coincidence," grunted Peter Haversley. "Pure coincidence."

"Well, I pray for all your sakes you're telling the truth," murmured Sam, wiping a weary hand across his ash-grimed face, "because the police aren't the only ones who'll be asking questions. The Lavenhams certainly won't stay quiet."

"I hope you're not suggesting that one of us set fire to that beastly little place," said Cynthia crossly. "Honestly, Sam, I wonder about you sometimes."

He shook his head sadly, wishing he could dislike her as comprehensively as Siobhan Lavenham did. "No, Cynthia, I'm suggesting you knew it was going to happen, and even incited the local youths to do it. You can argue that you wanted revenge for Lavinia and Dorothy's deaths, but aiding and abetting any crime is a prosecutable offence and"—he sighed—"you'll get no sympathy from me if you go to prison for it."

Behind them, in the hall of Malvern House, the telephone began to ring. . . .

Wednesday, 10th February, 1999

Siobhan had put an opened envelope on the desk in front of the detective inspector. "Even if Patrick is the murderer and even if Bridey knows he is, it doesn't excuse this kind of thing," she said. "I can't prove it came from Cynthia Haversley, but I'm a hundred percent certain it did. She's busting a gut to make life so unpleasant for Liam and Bridey that they'll leave of their own accord."

The inspector frowned as he removed a folded piece of paper and read the letters pasted onto it.

HAnGInG IS Too GOoD foR THE LikEs of YOU.

BUrN in h e l l

"Who was it sent to?" he asked.
"Bridey."
"Why did she give it to you and not to the police?"

"Because she knew I was coming here today and asked me to bring it with me. It was posted through her letterbox sometime the night before last."

("They'll take more notice of you than they ever take of me," the old woman had said, pressing the envelope urgently into Siobhan's hands. "Make them understand we're in danger before it's too late.")

He turned the envelope over. "Why do you think it came from Mrs. Haversley?"

Feminine intuition, thought Siobhan wryly. "Because the letters that make up 'hell' have been cut from a *Daily Telegraph* banner imprint. It's the only broadsheet newspaper that has an 'h,' an 'e,' and two 'l's in its title, and Cynthia takes the *Telegraph* every day."

"Along with how many other people in Sowerbridge?"

She smiled slightly. "Quite a few, but no one else has Cynthia Haversley's poisonous frame of mind. She loves stirring. The more she can work people up, the happier she is. It gives her a sense of importance to have everyone dancing to her tune."

"You don't like her." It was a statement rather than a question.

"No."

"Neither do I," admitted the inspector, "but it doesn't make her guilty, Mrs. Lavenham. Liam and/or Bridey could have acquired a *Telegraph* just as easily and sent this letter to themselves."

"That's what Bridey told me you'd say."

"Because it's the truth?" he suggested mildly. "Mrs. Haversley's a fat, clumsy woman with fingers like sausages, and if she'd been wearing gloves the whole exercise would have been impossible. This"—he touched the letter—"is too neat. There's not a letter out of place."

"Peter then."

"Peter Haversley's an alcoholic. His hands shake."

"Jeremy Jardine?"

"I doubt it. Poison-pen letters are usually written by women. I'm sorry, Mrs. Lavenham, but I can guarantee the only fingerprints I will find on this—other than yours and mine, of course—are Bridey O'Riordan's. Not because the person who did it wore gloves, but because Bridey did it herself."

01:10 A.M.—*Tuesday, 9th March, 1999*

Dr. Bentley clicked his tongue in concern as he glanced past Cynthia to her husband. Peter was walking unsteadily towards them after answering the telephone, his face leeched of colour in the lights of the fire engines. "You should be in bed, man. We should all be in bed. We're too old for this sort of excitement."

Peter Haversley ignored him. "That was Siobhan," he said jerkily. "She wants me to tell the police that Rosheen is missing. She said Liam called the farm from Kilkenny Cottage at eight-thirty this evening, and she's worried he and Rosheen were in there when the fire started."

"They can't have been," said Jeremy.

"How do you know?"

"We watched Liam and Bridey leave for Winchester this morning."

"What if Liam came back to protect his house? What if he phoned Rosheen and asked her to join him?"

"Oh, for God's sake, Peter!" snapped Cynthia. "It's just Siobhan trying to make trouble again. You know what she's like."

"I don't think so. She sounded very distressed." He looked around for a policeman. "I'd better report it."

But his wife gripped his arm to hold him back. "No," she said viciously. "Let Siobhan do her own dirty work. If she wants to employ a slut to look after her children then it's her responsibility to keep tabs on her, not ours."

There was a moment of stillness while Peter searched her face in appalled recognition that he was looking at a stranger, then he drew back his hand and slapped her across the face. "Whatever depths you may have sunk me to," he said, "I am *not* a murderer. . . ."

***LATE NEWS—The Telegraph—Tuesday,
9th March, A.M.*

Irish Family Burnt Out
by Vigilantes

The family home of Patrick O'Riordan, currently on trial for the murder of Lavinia Fanshaw and Dorothy Jenkins, was burnt to the ground last night in what police suspect was a deliberate act of arson. Concern has been expressed over the whereabouts of O'Riordan's elderly parents, and some reports suggest bodies were recovered from the gutted kitchen. Police are refusing to confirm or deny the rumours. Suspicion has fallen on local vigilante groups who have been conducting a "hate" campaign against the O'Riordan family. In face of criticism, Hampshire police have restated their policy of zero tolerance towards anyone who decides to take the law into his own hands. "We will not hesitate to prosecute," said a spokesman. "Vigilantes should understand that arson is a very serious offence."

6.

Tuesday, 9th March, 1999

When Siobhan heard a car pull into the driveway at 6:00 A.M. she prayed briefly, but with little hope, that someone had found Rosheen and brought her home. Hollow-eyed from lack of sleep, she opened her front door and stared at the two policemen on her doorstep. They looked like ghosts in the grey dawn light. Harbingers of doom, she thought, reading their troubled expressions. She recognised one of them as the detective inspector and the other as the young constable who had flagged her down the previous night. "You'd better come in," she said, pulling the door wide.

"Thank you."

She led the way into the kitchen and dropped onto the cushion in front of the Aga again, cradling Patch in her arms. "This is Bridey's dog," she told them, stroking his muzzle. "She adores him. *He* adores her. The trouble is he's a hopeless guard dog. He's like Bridey"—tears of exhaustion sprang into her eyes—"not overly bright—not overly brave—but as kind as kind can be."

The two policemen stood awkwardly in front of her, unsure where to sit or what to say.

"You look terrible," she said unevenly, "so I presume you've come to tell me Rosheen is dead."

"We don't know yet, Mrs. Lavenham," said the inspector, turning a chair to face her and lowering himself onto it. He gestured to the young constable to do the same. "We found a body in the kitchen area, but it'll be some time before—" He paused, unsure how to continue.

"I'm afraid it was so badly burnt it was unrecognisable. We're waiting on the pathologist's report to give us an idea of the age and"—he paused again—"sex."

"Oh, God!" she said dully. "Then it must be Rosheen."

"Why don't you think it's Bridey or Liam?"

"Because . . ." She broke off with a worried frown, "I assumed the phone call was a hoax to frighten Rosheen. Oh, my God! Aren't they in Winchester?"

He looked troubled. "They were escorted to a safe house at the end of yesterday's proceedings but it appears they left again shortly afterwards. There was no one to monitor them, you see. They had a direct line through to the local police station and we sent out regular patrols during the night. We were worried about trouble coming from outside, not that they might decide to return to Kilkenny Cottage without telling us." He rubbed a hand around his jaw. "There are recent tire marks up at the manor. We think Liam may have parked his Ford there in order to push Bridey across the lawn and through the gate onto the footpath beside Kilkenny Cottage."

She shook her head in bewilderment. "Then why didn't you find three bodies?"

"Because the Estate isn't there now, Mrs. Lavenham, and whoever died in Kilkenny Cottage probably died at the hands of Liam O'Riordan."

Wednesday, 10th February, 1999

She had stood up at the end of her interview with the inspector. "Do you know what I hate most about the English?" she told him.

He shook his head.

"It never occurs to you, you might be wrong." She placed her palm on the poison-pen letter on his desk. "But you're wrong about this. Bridey cares about my opinion—she cares about *me*—not just as a fellow Irishwoman but as the employer of her niece. She'd never do anything to jeopardise Rosheen's position in our house, because Rosheen and I are her only lifeline in Sowerbridge. We shop for her, we do our best to protect her, and we welcome her to the farm when things get difficult. Under no circumstances *whatsoever* would Bridey use me to pass on falsified evidence, because she'd be too afraid I'd wash my hands of her and then persuade Rosheen to do the same."

"It may be true, Mrs. Lavenham, but it's not an argument you could ever use in court."

"I'm not interested in legal argument, Inspector, I'm only interested in persuading you that there is a terror campaign being waged against the O'Riordans in Sowerbridge and that their lives are in danger." She watched him shake his head. "You haven't listened to a word I've said, have you? You just think I'm taking Bridey's side because I'm Irish."

"Aren't you?"

"No." She straightened with a sigh. "Moral support is alien to Irish culture, Inspector. We only really enjoy fighting with each other. I thought every Englishman knew that. . . ."

Tuesday, 9th March, 1999

The news that Patrick O'Riordan's trial had been adjourned while police investigated the disappearance of his parents and his cousin was broadcast across the networks at noon, but Siobhan switched off the radio before the names could register with her two young sons.

They had sat wide-eyed all morning watching a procession of policemen traipse to and from Rosheen's bedroom in search of anything that might give them a lead to where she had gone. Most poignantly, as far as Siobhan was concerned, they had carefully removed the girl's hairbrush, some used tissues from the wastepaper basket, and a small pile of dirty washing in order to provide the pathologist with comparative DNA samples.

She had explained to the boys that Rosheen hadn't been in the house when she got back the previous night, and because she was worried about it she had asked the police to help find her.

"She went to Auntie Bridey's," said six-year-old James.

"How do you know, darling?"

"Because Uncle Liam phoned and said Auntie Bridey wasn't feeling very well."

"Did Rosheen tell you that?"

He nodded. "She said she wouldn't be long but that I had to go to sleep. So I did."

She dropped a kiss on the top of his head. "Good boy."

He and Oliver were drawing pictures at the kitchen table, and James suddenly dragged his pencil to and fro across the page to obliterate what he'd been doing. "Is it because Uncle Patrick killed that lady?" he asked her.

Siobhan searched his face for a moment. *The rules had been very clear. . . . "Whatever else you do, Rosheen, please do not tell the children what Patrick has been accused of."* . . . "I didn't know you knew about that," she said lightly.

"Everyone knows," he told her solemnly. "Uncle Patrick's a monster and ought to be strung up."

"Goodness!" she exclaimed, forcing a smile to her lips. "Who said that?"

"Kevin."

Anger tightened like knots in her chest. *Ian had laid it on the line following the incident in the barn. . . . "You may see Kevin in your spare time, Rosheen, but not when you're in charge of the children." . . . "Kevin Wyllie? Rosheen's friend?"* She squatted down beside him, smoothing a lock of hair from his forehead. "Does he come here a lot?"

"Rosheen said we weren't to tell."

"I don't think she meant you musn't tell me, darling."

James wrapped his thin little arms round her neck and pressed his cheek against hers. "I think she did, Mummy. She said Kevin would rip her head off if we told you and Daddy anything."

Later—Tuesday, 9th March, 1999

"I can't believe I let this happen," she told the inspector, pacing up and down her drawing room in a frenzy of movement. "I should have listened to Ian. He said Kevin was no good the minute he saw him."

"Calm down, Mrs. Lavenham," he said quietly. "I imagine your children can hear every word you're saying."

"But why didn't Rosheen tell me Kevin was threatening her? God knows, she should have known she could trust me. I've bent over backwards to help her and her family."

"Perhaps that's the problem," he suggested. "Perhaps she was worried about laying any more burdens on your shoulders."

"But she was responsible for my *children*, for God's sake! I can't believe she'd keep quiet while some low-grade neanderthal was terrorising her."

The inspector watched her for a moment, wondering how much to tell her. "Kevin Wyllie is also missing," he said abruptly. "We're collecting DNA samples from his bedroom because we think the body at Kilkenny Cottage is his."

Siobhan stared at him in bewilderment. "I don't understand."

He gave a hollow laugh. "The one thing the pathologist can be certain about, Mrs. Lavenham, is that the body was upright when it died."

"I still don't understand."

He looked ill, she thought, as he ran his tongue across dry lips. "We're working on the theory that Liam, Bridey, and Rosheen appointed themselves judge, jury, and hangman before setting fire to Kilkenny Cottage in order to destroy the evidence."

***The Telegraph—Wednesday, 10th March,* A.M.

Couple Arrested

Two people, believed to be the parents of Patrick O'Riordan, whose trial at Winchester Crown Court was adjourned two days ago, were arrested on suspicion of murder in Liverpool yesterday as they attempted to board a ferry to Ireland. There is still no clue to the whereabouts of their niece Rosheen, whose family lives in County Donegal. Hampshire police have admitted that the Irish guardee have been assisting them in their search for the missing family. Suspicion remains that the body found in Kilkenny Cottage was that of Sowerbridge resident Kevin Wyllie, 28, although police refuse to confirm or deny the story.

04:00 A.M.—Thursday, 11th March, 1999

Siobhan had lain awake for hours, listening to the clock on the bedside table tick away the seconds. She heard Ian come in at two o'clock and tiptoe into the spare room, but she didn't call out to tell him she was awake. There would be time enough to say sorry tomorrow. Sorry for dragging him home early . . . sorry for saying Lavenham Interiors could go down the drain for all she cared . . . sorry for getting everything so wrong . . . sorry for blaming the English for the sins of the Irish . . .

Grief squeezed her heart every time she thought about Rosheen. But it was a complicated grief that carried shame and guilt in equal proportions, because she couldn't rid herself of responsibility for what the girl had done. "I thought she was keen on Kevin," she told the inspector that afternoon. "Ian never understood the attraction, but I did."

"Why?" he asked with a hint of cynicism. "Because it was a suitable match? Because Kevin was the same class as she was?"

"It wasn't a question of class," she protested.

"Wasn't it? In some ways you're more of a snob than the English, Mrs. Lavenham. You forced Rosheen to acknowledge her relationship with Liam and Bridey because *you* acknowledged them," he told her brutally, "but it really ought to have occurred to you that a bright girl like her would have higher ambitions than to be known as the niece of Irish gypsies."

"Then why bother with Kevin at all? Wasn't he just as bad?"

The inspector shrugged. "What choice did she have? How many unattached men are there in Sowerbridge? And you had to believe she was with someone, Mrs. Lavenham, otherwise you'd have started asking awkward questions. Still"—he paused—"I doubt the poor lad had any idea just how much she loathed him."

"No one did," said Siobhan sadly. "Everyone thought she was besotted with him after the incident in the barn."

"She was playing a long game," he said slowly, "and she was very good at it. You never doubted she was fond of her aunt and uncle."

"I believe what she told me."

He smiled slightly. "And you were determined that everyone else should believe it as well."

Siobhan looked at him with stricken eyes. "Oh God! Does that make it my fault?"

"No," he murmured. "Mine. I didn't take you seriously when you said the Irish only really enjoy fighting each other."

03:00 P.M.—*Thursday, 11th March, 1999*

Cynthia Haversley opened her front door a crack. "Oh, it's you," she said with surprising warmth. "I thought it was another of those beastly journalists."

Well, well! How quickly times change, thought Siobhan ruefully as she stepped inside. Not so long ago Cynthia had been inviting those same "beastly" journalists into Malvern House for cups of tea while she regaled them with stories about the O'Riordans' iniquities. She nodded to Peter, who was standing in the doorway to the drawing room. "How are you both?"

It was three days since she had seen them, and she was surprised by how much they had aged. Peter, in particular, looked haggard and grey, and she assumed he must have been hitting the bottle harder than usual. He made a rocking motion with his hand. "Not too good. Rather ashamed about the way we've all been behaving, if I'm honest."

Cynthia opened her mouth to say something, but clearly thought better of it. "Where are the boys?" she asked instead.

"Nora's looking after them for me."

"You should have brought them with you. I wouldn't have minded."

Siobhan shook her head. "I didn't want them to hear what I'm going to say to you, Cynthia."

The woman bridled immediately. "You can't blame—"

"Enough!" snapped Peter, cutting her short and stepping to one side. "Come into the drawing room, Siobhan. How's Ian bearing up? We saw he'd come home."

She walked across to the window from where she could see the remains of Kilkenny Cottage. "Tired," she answered. "He didn't get back till early this morning and he had to leave again at crack of dawn for the office. We've got three contracts on the go and they're all going pear-shaped because neither of us has been there."

"It can't be easy for you."

"No," she said slowly, "it's not. Ian was supposed to stay in Italy till Friday, but as things are . . ." She paused. "Neither of us can be in two places at once, unfortunately." She turned to look at them. "And I can't leave the children."

"I'm sorry," said Peter.

She gave a small laugh. "There's no need to be. I do rather like them, you know, so it's no hardship having to stay at home. I just wish it hadn't had to happen this way." She folded her arms and studied Cynthia curiously. "James told me an interesting story yesterday," she said. "I assume it's true, because he's a truthful child, but I thought I'd check it with you anyway. In view of everything that's happened, I'm hesitant to accept anyone's word on anything. Did you go down to the farm one day and find James and Oliver alone?"

"I saw Rosheen leave," she said, "but I knew no one was there to look after them because I'd been—well—watching the drive that morning." She puffed out her chest in self-defence. "I told you she was deceitful and lazy but you wouldn't listen to me."

"Because you never told me why," said Siobhan mildly.

"I assumed you knew and that it didn't bother you. Ian made no secret of how angry he was when you came home one night and found her with Kevin in the barn,

204

but you just said he was overreacting." She considered the wisdom of straight-speaking, decided it was necessary, and took a deep breath. "If I'm honest, Siobhan, you even seemed to find it rather amusing. I never understood why. Personally, I'd have sacked her on the spot and looked for someone more respectable."

Siobhan shook her head. "I thought it was a one-off. I didn't realise she'd been making a habit of it."

"She was too interested in sex not to, my dear. I've never seen anyone so shameless. More often than not, she'd leave your boys with Bridey if it meant she could have a couple of hours with Kevin Wyllie. Many's the time I watched her sneak into Kilkenny Cottage only to sauce out again five minutes later without them. And then she'd drive off in your Range Rover, bold as brass, with that unpleasant young man beside her. I did wonder if you knew what your car was being used for."

"You should have told me."

Cynthia shook her head. "You wouldn't have listened."

"In fact, Cynthia tried several times to broach the subject," said Peter gently, "but on each occasion you shot her down in flames and all but accused her of being an anti-Irish bigot."

"I never had much choice," murmured Siobhan without hostility. "Could you not have divorced Rosheen from Liam, Bridey, and Patrick, Cynthia? Why did every conversation about my nanny have to begin with a diatribe against her relatives?"

There was a short, uncomfortable silence.

Siobhan sighed. "What I really don't understand is why you should have thought I was the kind of mother who wouldn't care if her children were being neglected?"

Cynthia looked embarrassed. "I didn't, not really. I just thought you were—well, rather more relaxed than most."

"Because I'm Irish and not English?"

Peter tut-tutted in concern. "It wasn't like that," he said. "Hang it all, Siobhan, we didn't know what Rosheen's instructions were. To be honest, we thought you were encouraging her to make use of Bridey in order to give the poor old thing a sense of purpose. We didn't applaud your strategy—as a matter of fact, it seemed like a mad idea to us—" He broke off with a guilty expression. "As Cynthia kept saying, there's no way she'd have left two boisterous children in the care of a disabled woman and a drunken man, but we thought you were trying to demonstrate solidarity with them. If I trust the O'Riordans with my children, then so should the rest of you . . . that sort of thing."

Siobhan turned back to the window and the blackened heap that had been Kilkenny Cottage. *For want of a nail the shoe was lost . . . for want of a shoe the horse was lost . . . for want of mutual understanding lives were lost. . . .* "Couldn't you have told me about the time you went to the farm and found James and Oliver on their own?" she murmured, her breath misting the glass.

"I did," said Cynthia.

"When?"

"The day after I found them. I stopped you and Ian at the end of the drive as you were setting off for work and told you your children were too young to be left alone. I must say I thought your attitude was extraordinarily casual but—well"—she shrugged—"I'd rather come to expect that."

Siobhan remembered the incident well. Cynthia had stood in the drive, barring their way, and had then thrust her indignant red face through Ian's open window and lectured them on the foolishness of employing a girl with loose morals. "We both assumed you were talking about the night she took Kevin into the barn. Ian said afterwards that he wished he'd never mentioned it, because you were using it as a stick to beat us."

Cynthia frowned. "Didn't James and Oliver tell you about it? I sat with them for nearly two hours, in all conscience, and gave Rosheen a piece of my mind when she finally came back."

"They were too frightened. Kevin beat them about the head because they'd opened the door to you and said if I ever asked them if Mrs. Haversley had come to the house they were to say no."

Cynthia lowered herself carefully onto a chair. "I had no idea," she said in an appalled tone of voice. "No wonder you took it so calmly."

"Mm." Siobhan glanced from the seated woman to her husband. "We seem to have got our wires crossed all along the line, and I feel very bad about it now. I keep thinking that if I hadn't been so quick to condemn you all, *no one* would have died."

Peter shook his head. "We all feel the same way. Even Sam and Nora Bentley. They're saying that if they'd backed your judgment of Liam and Bridey instead of sitting on the fence—" He broke off on a sigh. "I can't understand why we allowed it to get so out of hand. We're not unkind people. A little misguided . . . rather too easily prejudiced perhaps . . . but not *unkind*."

Siobhan thought of Jeremy Jardine. Was Peter including Lavinia's grandson in this general absolution? she wondered.

7.

09:00 A.M.—Friday, 12th March, 1999

"Can I get you a cup of tea, Bridey?" asked the inspector as he came into the interview room.

The old woman's eyes twinkled mischievously. "I'd rather have a Guinness."

He laughed as he pulled out a chair. "You and Liam both. He says it's the first time he's been on the wagon since his last stretch in prison nearly twenty years ago." He studied her for a moment. "Any regrets?"

"Only the one," she said. "That we didn't kill Mr. Jardine as well."

"No regrets about killing Rosheen?"

"Why would I have?" she asked him. "I'd crush a snake as easily. She taunted us with how clever she'd been to kill two harmless old ladies and then have my poor Patrick take the blame. And all for the sake of marrying a rich man. I should have recognised her as the devil the first day I saw her."

"How did you kill her?"

"She was a foolish girl. She thought that because I'm in a wheelchair she had nothing to fear from me, when, of course, every bit of strength I have is in my arms. It was Liam she was afraid of, but she should have remembered that Liam hasn't been able to hurt a fly these fifteen years." She smiled as she released the arm of her wheelchair and held it up. The two metal prongs that located it in the chair's framework protruded from each end. "I can only shift myself to a bed or a chair when this is removed, and it's been lifted out that many times the ends are like razors. Perhaps I'd not have brought it down on her wicked head if she hadn't laughed and called us illiterate Irish bastards. Then again, perhaps I would. To be sure, I was angry enough."

"Why weren't you angry with Kevin?" he asked curiously. "He says he was only there that night because he'd been paid to set fire to your house. Why didn't you kill him, too? He's making no bones about the fact that he and his friends have been terrorising you for months."

"Do you think we didn't know that? Why would we go back to Kilkenny Cottage in secret if it wasn't to catch him and his friends red-handed and make you coppers sit up and take notice of the fearful things they've been doing to us these many months? As Liam said, fight fire with fire. Mind, that's not to say we wanted to kill them—give them a shock, maybe."

"But only Kevin turned up?"

She nodded. "Poor greedy creature that he is. Would he share good money with his friends when a single match would do the business? He came creeping in with his petrol can and I've never seen a lad so frightened as when Liam slipped the noose about his throat and called to me to switch on the light. We'd strung it from the beams and the lad was caught like a fly on a web. Did we tell you he wet himself?"

"No."

"Well, he did. Pissed all over the floor in terror."

"He's got an inch-wide rope burn round his neck, Bridey. Liam must have pulled the noose pretty tight for that, so perhaps Kevin thought you were going to hang him?"

"Liam hasn't the strength to pull anything tight," she said matter-of-factly, slotting the chair arm back into its frame. "Not these fifteen years."

"So you keep saying," murmured the inspector.

"I expect Kevin will tell you he slipped and did it himself. He was that frightened he could hardly keep his feet, but at least it meant we knew he was telling the truth. He could have named anybody . . . Mrs. Haversley . . . Mr. Jardine . . . but instead he told us it was our niece who had promised him a hundred quid if he'd burn Kilkenny Cottage down and get us out of her hair for good."

"Did he also say she had been orchestrating the campaign against you?"

"Oh, yes," she murmured, staring past him as her mind replayed the scene in her head. "'She calls you thieving Irish trash,' he said, 'and hates you for your cheap, common ways and your poverty. She wants rid of you from Sowerbridge because people will never treat her right until you're gone.'" She smiled slightly. "So I told him I didn't blame her, that it can't have been easy having her cousin arrested for murder and her aunt and uncle treated like lepers"—she paused to stare at her hands—"and he said Patrick's arrest had nothing to do with it."

"Did he explain what he meant?"

"That she hated us from the first day she met us."
She shook her head. "Though, to be sure, I don't know
what we did to make her think so badly of us."

"You lied to your family, Bridey. We've spoken to her
brother. According to him, her mother filled her head with
stories about how rich you and Liam were and how you'd
sold your business in London to retire to a beautiful cottage in a beautiful part of England. I think the reality must
have been a terrible disappointment to her. According to
her brother, she came over from Ireland with dreams of
meeting a wealthy man and marrying him."

"She was wicked through and through, Inspector, and
I'll not take any of her fault on me. I was honest with her
from the beginning. We are as you see us, I said, because
God saw fit to punish us for Liam and Patrick's wrongdo-
ing, but you'll never be embarrassed by it, because no one
knows. We may not be as rich as you hoped, but we're
loving, and there'll always be a home for you here if the
job doesn't work out with Mrs. Lavenham."

"Now Mrs. Lavenham's blaming herself, Bridey. She
says if she'd spent less time at the office and more time
with Rosheen and the children, no one would have died."

Distress creased Bridey's forehead. "It's always the
same when people abandon their religion. Without God

in their lives, they quickly lose sight of the devil. Yet for you and me, Inspector, the devil exists in the hearts of the wicked. Mrs. Lavenham needs reminding that it was Rosheen who betrayed this family . . . and only Rosheen."

"Because you gave her the means when you told her about Patrick's conviction."

The old woman's mouth thinned into a narrow line. "And she used it against him. Can you believe that I never once questioned why those poor old ladies were killed with Patrick's hammer? Would you not think—knowing my boy was innocent—that I'd have put two and two together and said, there's no such thing as coincidence?"

"She was clever," said the inspector. "She made everyone believe she was only interested in Kevin Wyllie, and Kevin Wyllie had no reason on earth to murder Mrs. Fanshaw."

"I have it in my heart to feel sorry for the poor lad now," said Bridey with a small laugh, "never mind he terrorised us for months. Rosheen showed her colours soon enough when she came down after Liam's phone call to find Kevin trussed up like a chicken on the floor. That's when I saw the cunning in her eyes and realised for the first time what a schemer she was. She tried to pretend Kevin was lying, but when she saw we didn't believe her, she snatched the petrol can from the table. 'I'll make you burn in hell, you stupid, incompetent bastard,' she told him. 'You've served your purpose, made everyone think I was interested in you when you're so far beneath me I wouldn't have wasted a second glance on you if I hadn't had to.' Then she came towards me, unscrewing the lid of the petrol can as she did so and slopping it over my skirt. Bold as brass she was with her lighter in her hand, telling Liam she'd set fire to me if he tried to stop her phoning her fancy man to come and help her." Her eyes hardened at the memory. "She couldn't keep quiet, of course. Perhaps people can't when they believe in their own cleverness. She told us how gullible we were . . . what excitement she'd had battering two old ladies to death . . . how besotted Mr. Jardine was with her . . . how easy it had been to cast suspicion on a moron like Patrick. . . . And when Mr. Jardine never answered because he was hiding in his cellar, she turned on me in a fury and thrust the lighter against my skirt, saying she'd burn us all anyway. Kevin will get the blame, she said, even though he'll be dead. Half the village knows he's been sent down here to do the business."

"And that's when you hit her?"

Bridey nodded. "I certainly wasn't going to wait for the flames to ignite."

"And Kevin witnessed all this?"

"He did indeed, and will say so at my trial if you decide to prosecute me."

The inspector smiled slightly. "So who set the house on fire, Bridey?"

"To be sure, it was Rosheen who did it. The petrol spilled all over the floor as she fell and the flint struck as her hand hit the quarry tiles." A flicker of amusement crossed her old face as she looked at him. "Ask young Kevin if you don't believe me."

"I already have. He agrees with you. The only trouble is, he breaks out in a muck sweat every time the question's put to him."

"And why wouldn't he? It was a terrible experience for all of us."

"So why didn't you go up in flames, Bridey? You said your skirt was saturated with petrol."

"Ah, well, do you not think that was God's doing?" She crossed herself. "Of course, it may have had something to do with the fact that Kevin had managed to free himself and was able to push me to the door while Liam smothered the flames with his coat, but for myself I count it a miracle."

"You're lying through your teeth, Bridey. We think Liam started the fire on purpose in order to hide something."

The old woman gave a cackle of laughter. "Now why would you think that, Inspector? What could two poor cripples have done that they didn't want the police to know about?" Her eyes narrowed. "Never mind a witch had tried to rob them of their only son?"

02:00 P.M.—*Friday, 12th March, 1999*

"Did you find out?" Siobhan asked the inspector.

He shrugged. "We think Kevin had to watch a ritual burning and is too terrified to admit to it because he's the one who took the petrol there in the first place." He watched a look of disbelief cross Siobhan's face. "Bridey called her a witch," he reminded her.

Siobhan shook her head. "And you think that's the evidence Liam wanted to destroy?"

"Yes."

She gave an unexpected laugh. "You must think the Irish are very backward, Inspector. Didn't ritual burnings go out with the Middle Ages?" She paused, unable to control her amusement. "Are you going to charge them with it? The press will love it if you do. I can just imagine the headlines when the case comes to trial."

"No," he said, watching her. "Kevin's sticking to the story Liam and Bridey taught him, and the pathologist's suggestion that Rosheen was upright when she died looks too damn flakey to take into court. At the moment, we're accepting a plea of self-defence and accidental arson." He paused. "Unless you know differently, Mrs. Lavenham."

Her expression was unreadable. "All I know," she told him, "is that Bridey could no more have burnt her niece as a witch than she could get up out of her wheelchair and walk. But don't go by what I say, Inspector. I've been wrong about everything else."

"Mm. Well, you're right. Their defence against murder rests entirely on their disabilities."

Siobhan seemed to lose interest and fell into a thoughtful silence which the inspector was loath to break. "Was it Rosheen who told you Patrick had stolen Lavinia's jewellery?" she demanded abruptly.

"Why do you ask?"

"Because I've never understood why you suddenly concentrated all your efforts on him."

"We found his fingerprints at the manor."

"Along with mine and most of Sowerbridge's."

"But yours aren't on file, Mrs. Lavenham, and you don't have a criminal record."

"Neither should Patrick, Inspector, not if it's fifteen years since he committed a crime. The English have a strong sense of justice, and that means his slate would have been wiped clean after seven years. Someone"—she studied him curiously—"must have pointed the finger at him. I've never been able to work out who it was, but perhaps it was you? Did you base your whole case against him on privileged knowledge that you acquired fifteen years ago in London? If so, you're a shit."

He was irritated enough to defend himself. "He boasted to Rosheen about how he'd got the better of a senile old woman and showed her Mrs. Fanshaw's jewellery to prove it. She said he was full of himself, talked about how both old women were so ga-ga they'd given him the run of the house in return for doing some small maintenance jobs. She didn't say Patrick had murdered them—she was too clever for that—but when we questioned Patrick and he denied ever being in the Manor House or knowing anything about any stolen jewellery, we decided to search Kilkenny Cottage and came up trumps."

"Which is what Rosheen wanted."

"We know that now, Mrs. Lavenham, and if Patrick had been straight with us from the beginning, it might have been different then. But unfortunately, he wasn't. His difficulty was he had the old lady's rings in his possession as well as the costume jewellery that Miss Jenkins gave him. He know perfectly well he'd been palmed off with worthless glass, so he hopped upstairs when Miss Jenkins's back was turned and helped himself to something more valuable. He claims Mrs. Fanshaw was asleep so he just slipped the rings off her fingers and tiptoed out again."

"Did Bridey and Rosheen know he'd taken the rings?"

"Yes, but he told them they were glass replicas which had been in the box with the rest of the bits and pieces. Rosheen knew differently, of course—she and Jardine understood Patrick's psychology well enough to know he'd steal

something valuable the minute his earnings were denied—
but Bridey believed him."

She nodded. "Has Jeremy admitted his part in it?"

"Not yet," murmured the inspector dryly, "but he
will. He's a man without scruples. He recognised a fellow
traveller in Rosheen, seduced her with promises of marriage, then persuaded her to kill his grandmother and her
nurse so that he could inherit. Rosheen didn't need an
alibi—she was never even questioned about where she was
that night because you all assumed she was with Kevin."

"On the principle that shagging Kevin was the only
thing that interested her," agreed Siobhan. "She *was*
clever, you know. No one suspected for a minute that
she was having an affair with Jeremy. Cynthia Haversley
thought she was a common little tart. Ian thought Kevin
was taking advantage of her. *I* thought she was having a
good time."

"She was. She had her future mapped out as Lady of
the Manor once Patrick was convicted and Jardine inherited the damn place. Apparently, her one ambition in life
was to lord it over Liam and Bridey. If you're interested,
Mrs. Haversley is surprisingly sympathetic towards her."
He lifted a cynical eyebrow. "She says she recognises how
easy it must have been for a degenerate like Jardine to
manipulate an unsophisticated country girl when he had
no trouble persuading *sophisticated*"—he drew quote marks

in the air—"types like her and Mr. Haversley to believe whatever he told thim."

Siobhan smiled. "I'm growing quite fond of her in a funny sort of way. It's like fighting your way through a blackened baked potato. The outside's revolting but the inside's delicious and rather soft." Her eyes strayed towards the window, searching for some distant horizon. "The odd thing is, Nora Bentley told me on Monday that it was a pity I'd never seen the kind side of Cynthia . . . and I had the bloody nerve to say I didn't want to. God, how I wish—" She broke off abruptly, unwilling to reveal too much of the anguish that still churned inside her. "Why did Liam and Bridey take Kevin with them?" she asked next.

"According to him, they all panicked. *He* was scared he'd get the blame for burning the house down with Rosheen in it if he stayed behind, and *they* were scared the police would think they'd done it on purpose to prejudice Patrick's trial. He claims he left them when they got to Liverpool because he has a friend up there he hadn't seen for ages."

"And according to you?"

"We don't think he had any choice. We think Liam dragged him by the noose round his neck and only released him when they were sure he'd stick by the story they'd concocted."

"Why were Liam and Bridey going to Ireland?"

"According to them, or according to us?"

"According to them."

"Because they were frightened . . . because they knew it would take time for the truth to come out . . . because they had nowhere else to go . . . because everything they owned had been destroyed . . . because Ireland was home. . . ."

"And according to you?"

"They guessed Kevin would start to talk as soon as he got over his fright, so they decided to run."

She gave a low laugh. "You can't have it both ways, Inspector. If they released him because they were sure he'd stick by the story, then they didn't need to run. And if they knew they could never be sure of him—as they most certainly should have done if they'd performed a ritual murder—he would have died with Rosheen."

"Then what are they trying to hide?"

She was amazed he couldn't see it. "Probably nothing," she hedged. "You're just in the habit of never believing anything they say."

He gave a stubborn shake of his head. "No, there *is* something. I've known them too long not to know when they're lying."

He would go on until he found out, she thought. He was that kind of man. And when he did, his suspicion about Rosheen's death would immediately raise its ugly head again. Unless . . . "The trouble with the O'Riordans," she said, "is that they can never see the wood for the trees. Patrick's just spent nine months on remand because he was more afraid of being charged with what he *had* done . . . theft . . . than what he *hadn't* done . . . murder. I suspect Liam and Bridey are doing the same—desperately trying to hide the crime they have committed, without realising they're digging an even bigger hole for themselves on the one they haven't."

"Go on."

Siobhan's eyes twinkled as mischievously as Bridey's had done. "Off the record?" she asked him. "I won't say another word otherwise."

"Can they be charged with it?"

"Oh, yes, but I doubt it'll trouble your conscience much if you don't report it."

He was too curious not to give her the go-ahead. "Off the record," he agreed.

"All right, I think it goes something like this. Liam and Bridey have been living off the English taxpayer for fifteen years. They get disability benefit for his paralysed arm, disability benefit for her broken pelvis, and Patrick gets a care allowance for looking after both of them. They get mobility allowances, heating allowances, and rate rebates." She tipped her forefinger at him. "But Kevin's built like a gorilla and prides himself on his physique, and Rosheen was as tall as I am. So how did a couple of elderly cripples manage to overpower both of them?"

"You tell me."

"At a guess, Liam wielded his useless arm to hold them in a bear hug while Bridey leapt up out of her chair to tie them up. Bridey would call it a miracle cure. Social services would call it deliberate fraud. It depends how easily you think English doctors can be fooled by professional malingerers."

He was visibly shocked. "Are you saying Patrick never disabled either of them?"

Her rich laughter pealed round the room. "He must have done at the time. You can't fake a shattered wrist and a broken pelvis, but I'm guessing Liam and Bridey probably prolonged their own agony in order to milk sympathy and money out of the system." She canted her head to one side. "Don't you find it interesting that they decided to move away from the doctors who'd been treating them in London to hide themselves in the wilds of Hampshire where the only person competent to sign their benefit forms is—er—medically speaking—well, past his sell-by date? You've met Sam Bentley. Do you seriously think it would ever occur to him to question whether two people who'd been registered disabled by a leading London hospital were ripping off the English taxpayer?"

"Jesus!" He shook his head. "But why did they need to burn the house down? What would we have found that was so incriminating? Apart from Rosheen's body, of course."

"Sets of fingerprints from Liam's right hand all over the door knobs?" Siobhan suggested. "The marks of Bridey's shoes on the kitchen floor? However Rosheen died—whether in self-defence or not—they couldn't afford to report it because you'd have sealed off Kilkenny Cottage immediately while you tried to work out what happened."

The inspector looked interested. "And it wouldn't have taken us long to realise that neither of them is as disabled as they claim to be."

"No."

"And we'd have arrested them immediately on suspicion of murder."

She nodded. "Just as you did Patrick."

He acknowledged the point with a grudging smile. "Do you know all this for a fact, Mrs. Lavenham?"

"No," she replied. "Just guessing. And I'm certainly not going to repeat it in court. It's irrelevant anyway. The evidence went up in flames."

"Not if I get a doctor to certify they're as agile as I am."

"That doesn't prove they were agile before the fire," she pointed out. "Bridey will find a specialist to quote psychosomatic paralysis at you, and Sam Bentley's never going to admit to being fooled by a couple of malingerers." She chuckled. "Neither will Cynthia Haversley, if it comes to that. She's been watching them out of her window for years, and she's never suspected a thing. In any case, Bridey's a great believer in miracles, and she's already told you it was God who rescued them from the inferno."

"She must think I'm an absolute idiot."

"Not you personally. Just your . . . er . . . kind."

He frowned ominously. "What's that supposed to mean?"

Siobhan studied him with amusement. "The Irish have been getting the better of the English for centuries, Inspector." She watched his eyes narrow in instinctive denial. "And if the English weren't so blinded by their own self-importance," she finished mischievously, "they might have noticed."